Knight of the Temple

Brennan Smith

ISBN: 1976384931
ISBN-13: 978-1976384936

INTRODUCTION

While searching for cool character names for what I hoped would be a great modern Islamic-terrorist thriller, I stumbled upon a fascinating but little known speech from the last Grand Master of the Knights Templar, and the words completely diverted my creative impulse.

No, not in some vain attempt to start a Crusade or reinstate the Templar order or anything. All I knew was that there was a great story behind his words, and I was going to find it.

This quest pulled me back through the Middle Ages to the Crusades, to the time of the Saracens, and all those European princes and highwaymen who sought their fortune in the Holy Land.

My schooling was spotty in general and woefully inadequate in this arena in particular. I assumed the basic narratives, that the Europeans were simply bigoted imperialists eager for a land grab, or that the church conned people into a Holy War with tales of a mystical Holy Grail, or that the Pope woke one morning and said, "Wait, what? Infidels in Jerusalem? Send in my armies!"

Elements of these may have been true. But to truly set the stage for our story, it's more important to understand that by the time of the Crusades, Islam had ruled Jerusalem for centuries. Its Christian and

Jewish population lived in relative peace by paying "tributes," or more precisely, extortion, to their Muslim rulers.

By this time, hordes of the Mohammedans had overrun much of Eastern Europe, the Middle East, and Africa. They crossed Gibraltar into Spain, sailed into France, pirated the Mediterranean, and demanded tributes from all over Christendom. They forced conversions, and enslaved or massacred those who stood in their way.

So when Pope Urban II heard that Christians and Jews in Jerusalem were being killed despite their annual tributes, he conceived of a daring, and not unsuccessful, counter-offensive.

The much maligned Crusades united the petty European kings under a common cause, and refocused the fight on a distant shore. In other words, like our own War on Terror, they wanted to "fight them over there so they won't have to fight them here."

A "crusade" by definition is a defensive assault against an already occurring evil. That alone might put this era under a different light, but medieval scholars also agree that without the Crusades, Europe would have been overrun and converted in that first great Jihad. We live in the third.

But my tale is not about Islam or even the Crusades. Their influence became incidental as I dove deep into the strange case of the Knights Templar.

That final speech by Grand Master Molay, delivered in 1314, was a revelation. It was profound, impassioned, and completely new to me...

Who were these Knights Templar, and of what were they accused?

I pressed hard into both the historical and apocryphal until this obscure medieval order became clear: the Poor Knights of the Temple of King Solomon, founded at the end of the first Crusade, dared both nobles and mercenaries to become warrior monks, the Jedi of their time.

By 1307 they had become the protectors of Europe, the first multinational banking organization, and the largest standing army in the world.

But in the following seven years, history reveals one of its most significant, untold events, one of mankind's largest man hunts, and one of history's biggest legal travesties, the implications of which resound through the centuries, even to this day.

And at its core, the arrest of one Jacque de Molay, who for seven long, torturous years, through thousands of legal proceeding, confessions, testimonies, counsels and executions, insisted that his knights were innocent.

For many it was a tale too unwieldy to relate.

For me, too big to ignore.

What many sources proffered as seven years of boring legal briefs, I saw as the untold tale of a young sailor in a sweeping, swashbuckling mystery adventure, a kind of legend that ignited the world's imagination throughout Europe centuries ago.

In fact, centuries later, in the French Revolution, as the crowd stormed the Bastille and beheaded King Louis XVI, as they dipped their fingers in his royal blood and waved to the crowds, their first proclamations were not, "Liberté! Egalité! Fraternité!"

They were, "Jacque de Molay, tu es vengé!"

That is, Jacque de Molay, you have been avenged.

Because this tale of the Knights Templar concerns their demise…

CHAPTER 1

Imagine languishing in the dank, claustrophobic filth of a prison cell in the year of our Lord 1305. And into this dim existence, the heavy door unlatched, creaked open, and spit the slim, balding priest, Esquiu de Florian, inside. He squinted back through the door's little window as his elegant voice implored, "At least let me see a priest!"

From behind him came a voice: "What profit is in that?"

Florian tried to refocus in the cell's darkness, finally offering: "Confession? The hope of heaven." Clearly, he didn't belong here, not among with this collection of cutthroats, thieves, and highwaymen in Toulouse Prison.

A figure stood and approached in the dim light. He was a sweaty Florentine pirate known here as Noffo Dei, sometimes Arnolfo Deghi, sometimes by other names entirely. His angular frame and predatory movement gave Florian the impression he might still have daggers ready for employment. "Confession?" he repeated.

"I was a priest," said Florian, retreating beside the wall, "For the Templars."

Noffo flashed a gruesome smile: "Then you can confess to me."

A raucous laughter erupted through the cell. Even Florian giggled nervously, until he realized that Noffo was not teasing.

While there were indeed examples of inmates confessing their sins to one another before their execution when priests were not available, Florian did not feel that he was on the brink of eternity. Not yet. He still had powerful friends, contacts to leverage. He had already written letters.

"Confession, good for the soul, eh priest?" Noffo continued, menacing toward him, "You might even survive the night. What would you confess?"

Florian swallowed, "Murder."

The snickering stopped. These inmates had known liars. And priests. And even priests who were liars. Florian did not appear to be one of them.

But the word was music to Noffo, who clapped his hands and embraced Florian as a brother. He put his arm around his shoulders, and led the priest toward a vacant corner where their whispers might not carry.

Florian relented, "So long as you don't betray a confidence. As I said, the Templars..."

Those words lingered. He was going to confess to murder, and it involved the Knights Templar.

Not that any in this poor fellowship knew what that meant. Little was known of the sacred order. Their history spread more like gossip and legend, and the Templars preferred it that way.

And what a gory pageant it was!

Every child knew the Crusades were full of follies and tragic circumstances, ultimately bringing about the fall of Jerusalem. If the tales are to be believed, by the year 1119, the blood ran up to the horses' bellies at the Temple Mount. Upon the ruins, a group of victorious

European mercenaries unearthed gold and exotic scrolls not seen since the Roman occupation. And there the sons of Europe conspired to make good of the bloody mess they had made.

One noted knight from among them spoke thusly: "Brothers! From this time forth, let us consecrate ourselves to protect these cities and the pilgrims that shall come to them! A holy order, ordained by God! Poor Knights of Christ and of this Temple of Solomon. Knights of the Temple!"

So it began, the first of a new class of warrior-monks that served the poor and fought to defend Christians on any shore. They were the fiercest in battle, eager to die for Christ as Christ had died for their souls.

England's Richard I, known as Richard the Lionheart, fought in later crusades and returned to retake his throne disguised in Templar vestments, the white cloth emblazoned with a red cross.

This Templar order grew into a vast multi-national organization, not just of soldiers, but of bankers, sailors, and serving brothers. They farmed their own lands, and fed themselves as well as the poor. They rescued Saracen slaves, returning them to Europe as free men.

Wealthy pilgrims to the Holy Lands could exchange their gold in the Paris Temple Bank for coded documents, a lambskin credit card that they would carry on safe Templar ships. Then in Jerusalem, the Temple Bank would decode the lambskin, and supply their wealth again.

Their diplomats resolved disputes between Christian and the Muslim countries, and from with these interactions, returned to Europe with scientific and scholarly knowledge gathered from as far as Alexandria and Babylon.

But in 1291, the tide turned. Saladin invaded, and the long Siege of Acre broke their spirits, and drove them from the Holy Lands.

Then arose the rumors and unanswered questions. Why had God allowed their enemies to drive them from His sacred ground? What hidden sin had corrupted these Poor Knights of the Temple? Had they simply grown lazy? Too rich? Something worse?

Every fat or drunk Templar was suspected of the foulest perversion. Even the Templar's habit of riding two on horseback, a physical expression of their perpetual poverty, was taken for sodomy. Their special codes began to look more sinister, their secret meetings and rituals more ominous.

Then Europe's nobility considered the strength of their numbers, the skill of their sailors, and the wealth of their banks. What could such a mass of corrupted nobles and mercenaries do, left to themselves without another crusade?

All this weighed on the grubby minds of these inmates of Toulouse, as Noffo led his new friend Florian into the corner. A Templar priest, confessing murder.

Some may have dismissed Florian's confession as another high-voiced prison lie, something to beguile the time, to keep himself alive and unmolested.

Some may have persisted in that opinion, except that moments later, Noffo sprang for the cell door, pounded it with his fists, and called into the echoing dark:

"Jailer! You must let me send a message! I have something vital to tell the king!"

CHAPTER 2

Far from these dank confines, across the great sea to the isle of Cyprus, a broken vessel drifted into port. And from its deck, up the planks to the solid rock, and up the stairs to the chapel, rose a barefoot, bronzed youth with singular determination.

He evaded the sentries with ease, scaled the wall like a monkey, and plunged into the chapel sanctuary, descending on a banner.

Only then did an old priest shout at him from the wings, and as guards entered, the youth darted to the white altar and clacked down his two most valuable possessions: a sword and a tattered scroll. Then he disrobed and lay naked, face down on the floor, arms extended like Christ on the Cross.

"I appeal for sanctuary," he shouted, "God, make me a Templar!"

The guards stood ready, though they didn't want to wrestle a naked youth away, while the old priest knelt beside him to ask, "Why would you come so –?"

"The Grand Master will approve me," the youth added, "Go. Tell him. Tell him Elias de Catalan is prepared to take the vows."

After another pause the old priest nodded, "And will you stay in prayer all night?"

"Let no one try to stop me," Elias answered.

And so they left him to his conscience, and the cold stone floor. There he lay all night confessing, exhausting his soul of every sin that he did not withhold.

Elias de Catalan, age 21. So must we believe, since like so many of this age, no record of him exists.

The Templars of Cyprus remembered him though, the boy among the mighty fleet. Elias had spent years rolling in and out of ports, serving where he could, listening to the tales of gallantry, the loss of comrades and the virtues of scripture.

But unlike most secular knights and nobles who come of age and thus "abandon their own wills… to wear permanently, the very noble armor of obedience," as the Rules of the Order state, Elias had no wealth or standing with his petition.

The religious orders turned away many applicants. Some came for security, some for fellowship, and others to lay down the weight of this world — renouncing titles, or wives, or the debts they owe.

Had the priest asked Elias why, he would have replied, "To become the hands of God in the world." He may not have known what the full significance or consequence of that phrase meant, but the possibilities kept him on his face all night.

No doubt the serving priests regarded him with some suspicion, given his appearance. No doubt they inspected his sword, possibly finding traces of gore in the cracks where the sea water and Elias' sharpening couldn't reach.

For certain, they inspected his scroll, and took their time, for as they discovered, this parchment was not a coat of arms, nor an introduction from any king.

It was his nautical map. Yes, these serving brothers, between vesper and matin prayers had the rare privilege of beholding a thing even more rare: a visual depiction of the world, laid out in vivid array. Jerusalem was at its center. Land masses were embroidered with exotic symbols and the faces of kings, beautiful women and caliphs. The vast Mediterranean lay dissected and detailed with handwritten notes. Its western edge, off Spain and the coast of Africa, showed dragons and tempests. The monsters of Gog and Magog held their siege at North and South poles.

Such a map would prove that this Elias de Catalan was no galley rat or deck hand, nor did he need a religious order to sustain a life. He could stand on the bridge of any ship worthy to be sailed, either as a merchant, captain, pilot, or pirate.

And as the priests discovered, Elias did indeed have the approval of the Grand Master. That was all he needed.

In the morning he took a bath for purity, heard mass, and took communion. Clothes and spurs were formally presented, as Sergeants and serving brothers instructed him on his duties: "to help the poor and weak, to respect women and show himself valiant and generous." The first of many mottos was to memorize "valour and generosity" in Latin.

Back in France, the vast, devouring organism of government had digested and delivered the Toulouse Prison confession into the king's hand.

King Philip the Fair was obviously handsome, and vain. Chroniclers insist that he was also a great sportsman, hunter and falconer, and the devoted husband to his Queen Jeanne, heiress of Navarre, until her death in 1305.

But more than anything, Philip was ambitious. He claimed that his inheritance was not merely France, but the insignia and holy mission of Charlemagne; that is, to be the champion of Christendom. To him, the monarchy and church were inseparable. To oppose him was not only treason but heresy.

Naturally this brought him into conflict with Pope Boniface VIII, who rebuked him for channeling church tithes directly into his own "crusades" against his political rivals. That argument ended with Boniface's premature death, and his successor, old Benedict XI, reasserted papal authority by excommunicating two of King Philip's chancellors (for reasons that will be obvious).

But by the advent the Toulouse prison confession, the tide had turned. Pope Benedict was also dead, and King Philip was busy coronating an old friend, Bertrand de Got, a French Bishop, who through political maneuvering was crowned Pope Clement V in Lyon Cathedral, in France.

On the fifth day of June in the Year of our Lord 1305, the trumpets blew, and hymns ascended for an entry procession of nobility that lasted for over an hour.

But by the time the golden papal tiara finally descended, the politics had begun.

There in the shadows, the king’s chancellor, Guillaume de Nogaret, with a hook nose like a bird of prey, dangled an official document, luring another humorless bureaucrat, the Archbishop Sens, out of his seat.

"Expecting a French Pope will lift your excommunication?" the Archbishop sneered, receiving the paper.

"I could always send him to Rome," Nogaret shot back, "The Italians would kill him of course, but that wouldn't be so long as eternity."

That was a threat. Everyone knew that the Italian Bishops were furious over Clement's election. France was not only his home, but his sanctuary.

The Archbishop let the threat pass while he read the paper. Each line pulled him closer to the page: "Against the Templars?"

"I have a signed confession and a witness," Nogaret added.

"Who? That… that villain Aldofo or something, the one you used to accuse the Bishop of Troyes?" The Archbishop tried to return the paper: "It was sorcery then, wasn't it?"

Nogaret shoved the paper squarely against the Archbishop's chest, "The King wants the Pope to make this his first priority."

"Even if it's true, how will you bring charges against them?" The Archbishop posed, his mind racing, "The Templars have the largest standing army in the world, subject to no laws, pay no taxes and answer only to..."

And his voice left him. He turned to the procession of nobles, each stooping, and kissing the French Pope's ring.

"I trust I can count on your support," said Nogaret.

"But, this is dangerous," said the Archbishop.

"We all have our duties, Archbishop. First, get the Pope to summon the Grand Master. Discreetly. Use whatever excuse you will, but get him to Paris."

The Archbishop whirled around, searching through the crowd. He hoped that the Grand Master might be in attendance so he could avoid this new responsibility.

But alas, he was far from that garish ceremony with its three-tiered tiara and side intrigues. He was in Cyprus, in a simple stone cathedral, filled with a light monastic hum, and a thousand Templar knights.

By the altar, as final vows on bended knees made newly minted knights, the grizzled Grand Master Jacques de Molay, age 62, like a proud father to all, presented Templar swords in the name of St. Michael and St. George to:

"Brother Aldo...

"Brother Xavier...

"Brother Elias..."

Yes, the born pirate became the hands of God, with a cheerful wink for his benefactor, and a new motto on his lips: "Spes mea in Deo est," meaning, "My hope is in God."

CHAPTER 3

So it came to pass within another year that the trumpets sounded in Paris for Grand Master Molay.

In this age, each district was alive and bustling, stamped with the character of the great trades, from tanners to smiths, each shop overflowing with excitement, and merchants hocking their wares with a cry.

Everything was proclaimed with criers in Paris. Booming voices delivered news, regulations, tax levies, auction sales, and of course, advertising. Come and buy!

The most popular: tavern criers, bellowing the virtues of their stock as they poured glass after glass. And in reply, the crowds in Paris bought and drank, and bought and ate, and danced with the minstrels, and bartered their possessions and ventured into any number of peculiar enterprises.

But on this October day, the merchants withdrew their wares from the street and the crowds parted for one great procession: imagine sixty mounted knights in arms, their vestments clean, their beards thick and helmets high, all attended by black robed squires and sergeants, their servants, and a train of 12 pack horses heaped with treasure.

And at this procession's head, Molay, in full regalia and flanked with banners.

The children swarmed, and rather than sit perched as a regal statue or stiff-necked general, the Grand Master played like a carnival showman. He waved as they waved. He patted the heads of youth, and plied them with riddles, as, "I can see you at any time, but you can only see me at night. What am I?"

"A star," Elias said, sniffing the air.

Molay flashed him a look of disapproval but Elias ignored it, casting a wary eye over the crowd: "Shouldn't we be in Poitiers, telling your riddles to the Pope?"

"Patience to our new pontiff, and you, Elias," Molay replied, expanding himself, "Paris is the height of everything! You may spend your whole life at sea, but you should see Paris once!"

The crowd cheered. The banners shook, and many Templars laughed in agreement.

But Elias kept studying the faces in the windows. The shadows on the rooftops.

Molay reached out and warmly touched Elias' arm, "I need to prepare you for peace. Ask me later about our ships at La Rochelle."

Elias smiled in spite of himself, "You are full of surprises, Grand Master."

Molay nodded, and returned to entertaining the children.

He was overdoing it, Elias thought. The procession was enjoyable, but unnecessary. Molay was already one of the most powerful men in the world. Who was he trying to impress?

Then he noticed a dark-haired young woman standing by an alleyway. She hadn't joined the parade. She wasn't waving or celebrating.

And something else: she was afraid.

But not of the Templars. On the contrary, she began to follow, brushing though the bustling humanity to keep between the banners, as if trying to be noticed by the Grand Master.

But then Elias thought: what if she was after his attention? After all, he was the youngest knight in procession, not much older than she was. His blood rushed to his cheeks as he allowed himself to recognize that she was beautiful. In fact, he had rarely seen so pleasant a face in all his life — not that that was saying much.

He dared to wonder that perhaps she thought that their eyes had met, and perhaps that drew her on. That he might conquer for her whatever fear she felt.

The criers clanging their ale and toasting the procession shook Elias back to his vows, to his new identity. As the Templar code read, "The company of women is a dangerous thing, for by it the old devil has led many from the straight path to Paradise."

So Elias blinked back his urges and concluded that the dark haired beauty must surely be a prostitute. Her masters must have threatened her with whipping had she not tempted into her snare the youngest, most gorgeous knight in procession. Him!

Could that be it, he wondered? That God was testing him? Or more likely, Molay was testing him, thrusting him into this sea of temptation for taking his vows of service and chastity so young, so boldly that the Grand Master could not refuse him without losing face.

Then what did Molay mean by seeing Paris once?

No, Elias chided himself. He must not dwell on such things. He knew the rumors of how lax, fat and wayward the Paris Templars had become. How Molay wanted to discuss discipline with the pope and change their reputation.

But that woman's fearful look! Her urgency! As if some warning wore on those perfect, slightly parted lips as she pressed though the crowd.

Elias then realized how many Parisians were looking where he was looking. He spun his head forward again, wincing: Lord have mercy! Not half an hour in Paris and caught leering at a prostitute! How easy it is for man to fall. He repented in his mind and yearned for his confessor. The order and its reputation must come first. He longed to redress each rumor with exemplary behavior, each whisper with firm Christian truth. And if necessary, any accusations with the back of his hand.

But then he didn't know where to cast his eyes. Settling on the merchant carts would imply that he's a glutton. To smile with the revelers would clap him a drunk!

Good God, why had Molay brought him to Paris?

Elias set his eyes on his Grand Master, who seemed oblivious to the moral struggle and their perceived condemnation. He continued, happily engaging the children with riddles without a care, it seemed.

But in all this, Elias failed to notice how Molay tilted his head with defiance as they passed the Parliament building. But it did not go unnoticed.

Hovering by the upstairs window, and turning on his heels, Chancellor Nogaret tore aside the curtains overhanging his bed, "Out!"

Two naked prostitutes rolled to their feet, pulling the sheets with them. As they dressed, Nogaret kicked the bed to spur their exit, and then stormed past his desk covered with formal papers, past the sitting area, and kicked open his private side door, which lead down a staircase to the street.

He stormed across the chamber again muttering, "Discreetly… So he enters Paris like a Roman general!"

He flung the hall door wide and wagged his finger at a sleepy government page leaning against the banners, "You! Find me the Archbishop! Go!"

The page fled down the ornate staircase, as Nogaret returned to his office and slammed the door. He exhaled to steady his rage.

"You think the Templars know?" Noffo's accent grated on the Chancellor's ears. His bulk also blocked the side exit, trapping the slower prostitute like a mouse. He nuzzled her hair as she waited silently to be released.

Nogaret directed with pursed lips. Reluctantly, Noffo opened his hand, and she disappeared.

"If the Grand Master knew he wouldn't have come," Nogaret said, "And you shouldn't have."

Noffo reached for a stoop of liquor from the side table, but again Nogaret intervened, dropping some money into Noffo's hand, and signaling toward the stairs with his chin.

Noffo weighed the coins in his hand: "For my service, the king –"

"Would pay you more? The king is Christendom's foremost advocate, Noffo. He must not see pirates like you."

"Who got that confession for you, eh? Who always gets?" Noffo pulled up his sleeve, showing an old scar, "This, this for Florian. In Toulouse. The other scar is lower; you don't want to see." He placed a head lock on an invisible adversary, "Another broken neck I had to do, for protection. Or you would have a dead priest and nothing for our king."

Nogaret opened the side door and scattered several coins down the steps: "Want more? Find me more, but do not linger. The Templars must have no hint of the justice we bring them on Friday."

CHAPTER 4

"Friday," Molay heaved, staring into the flickering hearth, "No time at all."

Outside the chamber, the Paris Templars bustled, wrapping up the daily work. The bankers completed transactions, marking coded entries with exotic symbols in their sheepskin ledgers.

In the vaults, they counted florins, and checked their ledgers.

Chamber after another, the meticulous work went on, down to one cleric inventorying a large hay wagon by the south gate. He puzzled over its crates, equipment and provisions, jotting down what he saw until a determined Sergeant strode by, and snatched the ledger away.

"Wait! These aren't accounted for," the cleric blurted out: "Sergeant, I haven't completed..."

He pursued the Sergeant straight into the Records Room, into the presence of the Grand Master, who received the ledger with a nod.

"But I," the cleric began, and stopped. Molay nodded back warmly, a movement expressing thanks, but also dismissal. The Sergeant smiled and stared, waiting for the cleric to take the hint.

Still hoping to be heard, the cleric shifted toward the third man seemingly warming himself by the hearth. But Master Gerard, head officer for the Paris Temple, didn't object. This stern, weather-beaten knight and former ship captain simply eyeballed him: "Carry on, brother."

The cleric turned and left without another word.

Molay handed the ledger to Gerard, and Gerard tossed it straight onto the stack of ledgers in the fire.

The Sergeant lingered a moment more, almost in reverence for his cleric's lost labor, and then cleared this throat and held out a message for Molay, "The archbishop requests a meeting with you and Chancellor Nogaret. Tomorrow."

Master Gerard snickered, "Postpone them until next week."

That was meant to raise the Grand Master's spirits, he thought. He hoped that would be sufficient answer for the Sergeant as well, but Molay didn't bite.

"You cannot stay, brother," Gerard said, "Yours was a grand entrance, and their request was expected, but we leave tonight."

Molay slowly shook his head, still considering.

"They won't hear you, Grand Master. The king just bought himself the papacy."

Molay sighed, "Brother Gerard..."

But Gerald wasn't finished: "God knows how many bribes he made to buy a French Pope, but from ordination until now, Clement he has been in Poitiers. You know as well as I, he will never leave France. That means he is at the King's mercy. And if he succeeds in condemning us –"

"How can he?" Molay interrupted, "They'll arrest a few hundred knights who won't fight them and know nothing. All the evidence goes with you." He glanced again at the hearth, "Or ends here."

"Then why stay?"

"Because I have never left the innocent to suffer wrong," Molay replied. "I can always demand an audience with the Pope. Tell him... what I can. Leave tonight, without me."

The matter was therefore settled, though not to Gerard's satisfaction. He huffed toward the door.

"Only do this for me," Molay continued, "Take Elias."

Gerard stopped short: "Elias? The youth? He doesn't know anything."

"Neither did I at 21, when I took my vows."

Gerard shook his head, "Then he's just another –"

"He's the son of Ramiro Moisés de Catalan," Molay said, the name bearing considerable weight. "He has many talents."

Master Gerard waited. They already had many capable sailors in La Rochelle, many en route, and many others like the Sergeant were staying behind to keep up appearances. Everything had been planned.

Molay's shoulders sagged, almost pleading: "He grew up on my ship, Gerard."

CHAPTER 5

Elias had no official duties at the Paris Temple. Molay all but demanded he take in the city, but he could not bring himself to play a tourist.

First he attended vespers. He filled his ears with hymns, then knelt and filled the confessional with his grand desire to restore the order's reputation in France, and ultimately to restore their glory in the Holy Lands.

He spoke of the dark-haired woman who followed their procession, and blessed her for her troubles since he was ill-suited for any another ministry.

His burden lifted, Elias ate supper in silence, and then patrolled the street. He scowled at the French Templars standing about boozing with the festively costumed revelers, and the mass of idlers who lingered to steal from distracted merchants closing their shops for the night.

Feeling idle himself, Elias joined the serving brothers welcoming widows and orphans at their tables. His eye finally settled on a grim-faced orphan, who sulked without a hope. Elias looped a rope around the boy, and tugged at him playfully. The startled orphan pulled back, his head still down, trying to release himself. Then with a quick flick of the wrist, Elias tangled him up, and hoisted him onto his back.

The boy kicked to no avail. Elias could have carried a barrel twice this lad's size straight up the main mast of the Grand Master's ship, so it was little work to spring over a serving table, balance along the top of several benches and finally plunk the lad down on a chair nearest the kitchen lights.

"Look here," Elias began.

The boy sprang up to escape but Elias stepped hard on the rope, jerking the boy back again.

Elias pulled his map from his waist pouch, and splayed it out before him. As expected, the boy's eyes lit on its color, its dragons and tempests. On Gog and Magog. "The world before you, lad," Elias said, "Where God instructs the winds, reins back the monsters."

The boy ran his finger over the images. Elias guided the boy's hand through the Straits of Gibraltar, along his ship's line to the coast of France, and up to Paris.

"Where he protects orphans like you. And me."

The boy glanced up into Elias' face.

Elias winked, "In such a world, who knows what miracles wait around every corner."

Around the corner, the Sergeant dragged our dark-haired prostitute from an antechamber, across the Paris temple grounds and shoved her into the street.

Elias straightened, recognizing her immediately.

Out in the street, Noffo also noticed. He had stolen a goat mask from the revelers, and by this time was pulling it off and on for comic effect as he gossiped and muttered bawdy Italian phrases among the idle Templars.

But seeing the woman, he instinctively worked his way toward her.

"Please, you must! You owe me!" She demanded.

The Sergeant snatched her quick again and whispered, "Stop or you jeopardize us all, woman." Then louder, "We can offer no more solace today, Corinne. Your pardon and God greet you."

The Sergeant let her go, and strode back toward the Temple.

Corinne took deep breaths, her face flushed. She glanced at some other Templars but they smirked back, unaffected. She then ducked her head and storming away before her private shame became a public spectacle.

Elias quickly tucked away his map, kissed the boy on the crown of his head, and strode off after her.

The returning Sergeant, spotted Elias en route and called, "Brother Elias!"

Elias ignored him and kept walking.

"Brother Elias," the Sergeant repeated, closing the distance between them, "Gather your things. You leave for La Rochelle, immediately." He pointed toward the large hay wagon by the south gate.

"If you French brothers have time for lechery," Elias responded, "I still have time to serve."

But he was not alone. Noffo caught up with Corinne first, balancing his liquor as best he could after so much imbibing, "They owe me too, the criminals."

Corinne tried to ignore him.

"What did they reject you for, Babylon?" Noffo continued, working his goat mask up and down, "Come, I can give you better business," and with that, Noffo groped her backside.

Corinne turned and slapped him across the face, almost knocking his mask away. She turned and scurried past a group of revelers, keeping her head down.

The revelers laughed. One tooted his flute, but before any could strike up a song, Noffo whirled back, crashing his beer stein into the nearest face.

The music stopped, and as the group focused on their fallen comrade, Noffo shoved past them. Several seconds later he spotted her heading toward the church. Pulling the mask over his face, he circled around the shopkeepers and shifted into the shadows beside the church, coming up on her blind side.

Corinne glanced back, and not seeing her stalker, began to relax. The sound of vespers soothed her nerves, but before she reached the door, Noffo sprung: one hand cupping her mouth, the other yanking her hair, like reins on a horse, steering her into the shadows.

She struggled until she felt his dagger press against her jaw line. One vicious movement and he might redraw her face or tear her throat out completely. She stiffened and sucked a long breath as he dragged her behind the church's buttress.

"What do they owe you, Babylon?" This time Noffo was insistent.

"You’re drunk!" She spat, barely moving.

"Drunk like a Templar, but they don’t make deals, not with whores. With boys maybe, the God-mocking sodomites."

Noffo withdrew his dagger for some new torture but suddenly, he flew back...

He lashed out at throat height, but Elias ducked, and yanked Noffo’s cloak again, toppling him into the church buttress.

He stepped between Noffo and Corinne, "What did you say about the Templars?"

Noffo measured the distance, "God knows, the devil knows, but I can keep it quiet for a price."

"You're full of words," Elias said calmly.

"A better Christian than any Templar!"

"We don't kill Christians," Elias said, and pointed his thumb at the church: "Take your slanders to confession."

Noffo's mask couldn't hide the slight smile that crept across his face. Unlike the other pudgy, corrupted knights of Paris, here stood before him a "pure" Templar — at least one who thought he was. And that meant he was ignorant.

Corinne took quick breaths, "He must know... about the arrest."

Noffo's smile vanished. He feigned away, and then hurled the dagger.

Elias reacted instinctively, shifting his weight to avoid the blade, but Corinne threw up her arms, and that's where the dagger stuck.

As she fell back, Noffo drew his sword and attacked. The young Templar would be the first of his trophies, he thought, as he thrust hard and straight.

That might have worked in a brawl with any other drunk. But Elias was more than sober; he was able. His sword had left its sheath a moment before Noffo found his. It was already rising as Noffo drew, and by the time Noffo's point reached Elias' torso, Elias was six inches to the right. He glanced off Noffo's blade and in the same fluid motion slammed his sword pommel into Noffo's mask.

Noffo crumbled to the ground, his sword falling free. Elias rushed over him, his eyes flashing with rage, sword poised for the kill.

"Good God, what did you do before you were a monk?" Corinne exclaimed.

Elias came to himself, the vesper hymn filling his ears. He then noticed that Noffo was motionless. The mask had split and blood poured from his brow. The battle was over.

Elias quickly sheathed his sword and examined Corinne's forearm. He could barely see anything in the poor light but fearing rusty steel against her flesh, he pulled the dagger out, and more blood came. He quickly rolled her sleeve over the wound and applied pressure, "You need a surgeon."

"No, take me out of France with you!" Corinne's expression was desperate, pleading; their faces pressed close.

Elias stopped short. He had looked away from her in the crowd, but now he found himself transfixed by her eyes, torn between temptation and confusion.

"Didn't they tell you?" She pressed, "Nogaret has orders to arrest you — all of you — on Friday!"

"Arrest the Templars? That's absurd. He doesn't have the authority –"

"I'm not lying. I'm the one that warned you!" Her eyes scanned his, "Those papers, the ones in the hands of every magistrate, for Friday? Please, wherever you're going..." She swallowed hard, tears welling up in her eyes, "Take me with you."

Elias blushed and looked away. He couldn't be here, hearing this from her. And what she said was too incredible. If Nogaret had planned an arrest, why would the Pope summon the Grand Master to Poitiers to discuss a new crusade with King Philip?

Oh! But then if the summons was to get the Grand Master to France, to answer charges against the Templars… Molay didn't go to Poitiers. He came to Paris, on purpose. But to what end?

"Does the Grand Master know?" Elias asked.

"Brother Elias?" The Templar Sergeant quickly approached, his eyes landing on Noffo, slowly stirring.

"Dear God, you sailors are always trouble." The Sergeant pulled Elias up, "Leave her. Get to the wagon!"

"She's hurt."

The Sergeant shoved Elias in the right direction, "Go! Grand Master's orders."

Elias took several steps toward the Paris Temple. He could see the hay wagon's silhouette in the torchlight as the rest of Paris fell dark.

But still that nagging question slowed him: could the woman be believed? Was the Grand Master in danger?

Elias glanced back and watched as the Sergeant shook his head at Corinne, and in disgust, stormed away, abandoning her again.

She groaned after him, her words failing. She got up and took several weary steps along the church's side, holding her bloody, quivering arm. Her eyes drooped and her head began to feel as heavy as her feet upon the stones.

Noffo managed to roll over, still several moments before finding his feet, but he would not be down for long.

Elias considered it all, and took another step toward the wagon, and another, his mind outpacing his steps: what if Corinne was right? What if Nogaret had indeed planned an arrest and Molay did not know?

But he was a man under orders. Under an oath of obedience. Get to the wagon.

"Move! Bring bandages and a surgeon!" Elias' voice echoed through the woman's ward of a hospital run by nuns.

A young sister hopped to, not knowing from whence the voice came. She grabbed an armful of cloth, enough to service a regiment, and turned to see…

Elias lowering a bloody and desperate Corinne onto a bed while she wailed: "You stubborn monk! If we don't run –"

"We'll fight them," Elias railed, forgetting his surroundings, "I know who Nogaret is. The Templars answer to the Pope alone."

An uncomfortable silence followed, before: "I thought, to remain pure, a Templar avoids even the face of a woman." That gentle rebuke came from a mother superior.

Elias lowered his gaze to Corinne's wound, "See? Can't take you anywhere." He nodded to the mother superior: "Keep her here as long as you can. Discreetly."

CHAPTER 6

The government page with message in hand bounded up the stairs of Parliament, and reached with hesitation for Chancellor Nogaret's chamber door. He screwed up his courage, knocked and entered, finding its occupants in mid-sentence:

"... Like a small dog yapping at a much larger one," Nogaret ranted, "And your proposal for the next Crusade?" He dumped a ledger at the Grand Master's feet, "Frankly, ever since you Templars lost the Holy Lands, the rumors – "

"Rumors?" Molay broke in, "We dispatch envoys for kings and priests for confession, but I would be summoned over rumors?" His voice quivered at the end to make the notion sound that much more absurd.

Very few would know the details of the presumed arrest and Molay knew he could not trick them out of the Chancellor. Nor could he let on too much, lest they discover that he had made preparations.

His proposal for a new Crusade was thick, finely displayed, and may have been genuine, especially if it succeeded in diverting the French purposes. Defending Christendom from the Mohammedans was the Templars' best defense.

The Archbishop Sens sat nearby: "Grand Master, it goes deeper…"

"If my French knights lack discipline…" Molay hung out that last word for mockery.

"How about the secret practices and meetings?" Nogaret said.

Secret practices, Molay thought? Perhaps he might yet pry something from them.

But the Archbishop continued: "Your envoys and priests would be little versed with those, and your temple masters defer to you. Regardless of our mutual regard, in such ecclesiastical matters, um…" he mulled over his next words.

"We have the right –" Nogaret assisted.

"We?" Molay taunted, glancing back at Nogaret and shifting in his seat, "Are you not still excommunicate for attacking Pope Boniface?"

"Grand Master," Archbishop Sens pleaded.

"Boniface was a heretic," Nogaret fired back.

The Archbishop dropped his gaze into his lap.

Molay slowly turned back to the Chancellor, "Anyone who disagrees with your king is your heretic. Perhaps it was neither for you nor his holiness that I was summoned." Molay paused, calmly folding his hands, "God knows the sad condition of our host, the church. Its inner feuds make these petty rumors of some indolent French knights quite pale in comparison."

Nogaret huffed, "You think God called you to Paris?"

"Perhaps I might prove some service between you and your confessor, Guillaume de Nogaret," Molay continued, "And perhaps I could help repair this rift our pontiff has with the Italians."

"If we might return to the matter," the Archbishop sighed, but Molay pounced:

"For a proper balance of power, Pope Clement should serve in Rome!" And with that, Molay sat back, triumphant. Nothing ended conversations in Paris more quickly than implying the Pope was a proxy for the King of France.

Molay then turned a gracious eye toward the embarrassed page, who as we recall, entered without being summoned and had since stood on tiptoe, unwilling to interrupt.

"Out with it," Nogaret helped.

"There is a Templar knight to speak urgently with the Grand Master."

Nogaret laughed, "Perhaps the Grand Master assumes too many responsibilities already."

The Archbishop shot Nogaret a look of disapproval as Molay retrieved his ledger from the floor, and rose to leave: "The world waits not for us, no matter what we command."

He made slight bows to them both, and then smirked toward the chancellor: "Though for a private wager among my officers, just how many Cardinals did the King have to bribe to get a French Pope?"

He turned to leave without an answer, but Nogaret couldn't let Molay have the last word: "Ten out of fifteen."

The Archbishop winced.

"Exploit what you can," Molay said, "The truth is, you can’t command the Pope to do anything."

Molay left, not pausing for response, though if he had, he might have caught Nogaret mutter under his breath, "Not yet."

Molay took the stairs heavily. Each step down was a prayer, a prayer that each conspirator would have misgivings and second thoughts that might forestall their terrible plan. Or at least reduce its severity.

As he reached the outer doors of Parliament, Molay reminded himself that he still had cards to play. He could prepare his remaining knights, perhaps draft some directives of reform to appease the local officials. He also had occasion to address King Philip himself, perhaps plant in his ear the promise of a new crusade. He could echo the king warnings of "heretics" in Flanders that only an invasion could cure. Yes, the king's vanity and the promise of Templar support just might save them.

Molay's face dropped when he found Elias waiting.

"Grand Master, I couldn't find you last night –"

"Why aren't you off to La Rochelle?" Molay blurted out, "It's two days hard ride!"

Elias rushed in and whispered, "There's rumor of an arrest, and more. I examined the vaults; ledgers are burned, men are missing –"

"And so should you! Good God, Elias, why have you chosen now to disobey me?"

"I don't understand."

"There isn't time!" Molay glanced back at Parliament, then pulled Elias toward his horse, "You've got to get to La Rochelle before Friday. That's my order to you."

Elias sensed the fear in his voice, and bristled. "Say the word and I will kill Nogaret."

Molay stared in wordless disapproval. Had he not listened at all? Had he already forgotten his vows?

Elias melted: "I am sorry, Grand Master. I will go."

Elias mounted, both wishing there were more time. But Molay couldn't risk it, and perhaps, if Elias knew what was to follow, he'd refuse to leave, oath of obedience or not.

CHAPTER 7

Elias rode as fast as the horse could carry, snaking along the countryside to La Rochelle. Two days hard ride. He set his objectives over each horizon, one after another, just as he had at sea. Each sign post helped him to track his progress, as if he were riding upon his father's map.

As a boy he had memorized the contour of every line. His father demanded it, since the map was their primary tool, beside a compass, and or course, their wits.

Captain Ramiro Moises de Catalan was respected in all Christendom, though these honors did not make him rich. Wars had diminished the family fortunes, keeping him where he loved to be: at sea.

"Have you found us, Elias?" His father's warm voice would roll across the deck, "Or have we fallen off the end of the earth?"

At age seven, the boy Elias covered the dragons and tempests of the North Sea with his left hand to keep them out of mind. He guided his right index finger along his father's route, along the coast of Aragon and Spain, stopping near Gibraltar. Enemy territory, but Elias was confident that this was the spot.

Ramiro trimmed the main sail, releasing the breeze, and then lowered the sail part way. As the ship settled, he stood over his son's shoulder and reviewed the map.

Elias smiled proudly, slowly removing his left hand from the page. Ramiro noticed but didn't mock his son's superstition.

He nodded approvingly at Elias' mark and patted his back while mischievously attaching a hook to Elias' belt. The hook attached to a rope that ran up the main mast.

Elias discovered this too late.

Ramiro turned the ship into the wind. The wind caught the sail. The sail flew up, taking Elias with it, swinging him across the deck, over the side and back again. Elias laughed the whole way.

"A fair reply for a world of miracles!" Ramiro beamed, pulling the rope, sending his boy to the top of the mast. "While you're up, check the rigging!"

But Elias' eye caught something else. Another ship appeared from around a cove, and unlike Ramiro, who was tacking, this other ship was full into the wind, bearing straight for them.

"Father!" Elias yelled, pointing at it.

They both knew immediately: pirates.

Elias descended to the deck, while Ramiro turned full into the wind. The few shipmates Ramiro employed scrambled to their positions as flaming arrows hit the mast.

Elias fell flat on the deck.

"Get below!" Ramiro ordered.

Elias obeyed, tucking himself among the cargo and crew bedding. And waited.

Shouts rang out, some from his father. None good. A crash of wood on wood told Elias that the main mast had failed. The ship settled on the waves.

Moments later, Elias envisioned sea monsters scraping their claws over the deck, and seizing his father. What he actually heard were the hooks from the pirate ship, locking onto their gunwales and pulling the ships together.

Pounding feet across the deck preceded the splash of men. Indiscriminate shouts echoed from mid deck while others came from off the side.

Then the splashing ceased.

Elias waited for his father's voice. Was it safe?

The moments ticked by until he could not bear it. He brandished his dagger and inched his way back. He poked his head up from the hold. The sunlight blinded him momentarily, but the pirate ship became visible, its hooks clutching their gunwales.

Several pirates worked the ropes at the mast, directed by a tall and slender Arab, with a pronounced widow's peak hairline. He scanned the horizon, and waved aggressively at his crew, luring Elias' eyes momentarily over the waves.

They bounced back to the mast as another pirate hoisted up Ramiro's form, bloody and limp.

Elias' breath left him. He could not scream, but merely stared in horror. His father was certainly dead. The other shipmates were gone except for one, whom the pirates prodded mercilessly, demanding the contents of the cargo.

Then they turned, and saw Elias.

Elias ducked, and raced through the hold. He darted over the crates, kicked up dust and plunged through tight spaces only a boy could go, surging toward the bow.

He heard more frustrated shouts, and the shoving of crates. He looped the end of a rope over a barrel and pulled it tight against the ship, and then plunged out of the slim hatch in the bow.

Dangling just above the water line, Elias held on. His fingers and toes clenched the rope and settled his weight on its knotted end, and there he swung gently. His tearful eyes shut. And he prayed.

The image of his father, bloody and hung like a sail, burned into his mind. He wept and could think of nothing else, not of the pirates on deck, not of the cold water lapping his legs, nor the pain in his feet and hands. Nor would he ponder how long he might hold on.

"Infidel!"

Elias woke. Time had slipped behind the waves and now in the declining sun another vessel overshadowed him.

"This is Ramiro's ship. Where is Ramiro Moisés de Catalan!" This voice came from an English cog ship, its deep hull bobbing beneath its white sail with a red cross.

Elias held his breath, and waited for the reply. He didn't have to wait long...

The pirates loomed over Elias and shot arrows at the cog.

The cog shot back.

Elias shut his eyes again as arrows flitted above, until he heard the voice again: "Jump! Swim to us!"

A younger Jacque de Molay waved and called at Elias while other sailors hurled hooks onto Ramiro's deck.

Elias refused to move. Perhaps he had held on so long he wasn't able, but he also knew what happened to sailors who tried to swim away from these pirates.

Molay frowned, and then joined his crew. They moved as a unit, pulling the ships together.

Then a burly, barrel-chested German Templar, Hugh Von Grumbach, lunged onto Ramiro's deck and heaved his massive sword against the foe. He wounded one and reposted against several more as two others chopped at the hooks securing the Templar ship.

Still others moved on the Widow Peak captain's commands, releasing the hooks from their own ship. They calculated rightly that they couldn't win in the fight but they might outrun the cog, if they could pull away.

So while other Templars surged on board, the pirates tactically retreated to their vessel and hoisted sail.

Molay's blade clanged against the Widow Peak's scimitar. The pirate parried well, retreating comfortably, marking inches across the deck. He feigned left, and stepped behind the main mast, which bought him seconds. He used them to plunge a torch onto Ramiro's fallen sails, setting the deck on fire.

Molay surged again, driving Widow Peak back but the damage was done. The pirate smiled at the growing flames, and then dove into the sea toward his ship.

Molay didn't have time to follow. He directed: "Man the pails!"

As the Templars threw water at the expanding blaze, Molay raced to the bow, reaching down toward Elias: "De Catalan! Come, boy!"

The terrified boy still didn't budge.

"Jesus, he's loyal as an Assassin!" Molay exclaimed, motioning for help.

Two sailors braced Molay's legs as he stretched down, and hauled Elias up as Hugh chopped the rope against the ship.

Molay cradled Elias on deck, but they could not stay. The evening breeze worked faster than the pails. Ramiro's ship was going to burn.

"Abandon her," Hugh ordered, reluctantly, shooing Templars back to their cog.

Moments later, Elias was on the cog, watching the only life he had ever known consumed in flames and the sea. Tears obscured his vision but his limbs slowly relaxed, releasing the stub of rope.

Molay simply rocked him in his arms, and said nothing.

Hugh directed the crew, then with a knowing glance to Molay, laid a hand on Elias, "Put your hope in God, little Assassin. You owe your life to the next Grand Master of the Knights Templar."

CHAPTER 8

The sun rose over a milky mist covered Paris on October 13, 1307. The king's army stood at the Paris Temple gates where a magistrate held one of many official documents impressed with the king's seal.

He split the wax, quickly read the contents and signaled the battering ram to commence.

In the chapel, Molay knelt in prayer, surrounded by his guards, the Paris Templars, their priests, serving brothers, bank tellers and a few clerics. He tried to ignore the terrible sound of the splintering wood, and the percussion of approaching feet.

Every head turned as the magistrate's words echoed in the rafters, "By order of the church and King Philip, we arrest all Templars herein!"

The king's soldiers crowded the chapel door, and as they entered, several Templars instinctively reached for their swords.

Molay rose, holding out his hand: "Don't. We will not disgrace ourselves by fighting our fellow Christians."

And so they bent their heads, and quietly laid down their arms.

Thus began what history records as its most unlucky day, more commonly known as Friday the 13th.

Elias smelled the sea air and saw hints of the ocean grey as he crested the hill overlooking port La Rochelle.

But the port was empty. The Bay of Biscay was calm and foggy, with no horizon upon which to see the ships.

"Dear God," he exclaimed, "The ships... The ships are gone!"

He rode on toward the port, his guilt at having failed the Grand Master quickly replaced by fear. He saw Templar serving brothers escorted under guard, and several mounted French knights pointing and then charging toward him.

His right hand clapped down on his sword, but then Molay's admonishment to "prepare for peace" tickled him. Despite the rumored arrest he still knew nothing about, he still considered himself as part of a protected class of warrior monks under the Grand Master's direct command.

"You," a lead knight shouted, "Dismount and disarm!"

Elias held up a hand to stay them as seven mounted knights encircled him. He withdrew the cape from his shoulders to show his vestment: "You can't arrest me. I'm a Templar. I have –"

"Kill him if he doesn't yield!" The lead knight ordered, menacing with his lance.

One knight hopped from his saddle and grabbed the bridle of Elias' horse.

"In God's name – are you murderers?" Elias exclaimed, pulling back on his reins. His horse lurched.

The lead knight lunged with his lance, slashing Elias' left arm.

Elias toppled down, and instinct took over. His sword was loose before his feet and knees found the soil. He side-rolled away from his horse, with his sword protecting his belly, and as the French knights closed in, Elias fended off their lances in one circular motion. He put his feet under him, set his knees straight, and did the unexpected.

The French knights assumed Elias would retreat, that he would back up, and so, find himself impaled on their points again. Backing up was what they wanted.

Elias lunged forward, splitting the lances and shoving past them.

Before the knights could react, Elias kicked one horse in the thigh, glanced off another sword blow and dive-rolled under a third steed's belly, breaking out of their circle.

He sprinted uphill toward the trees. He had been riding so long, tension stiffened his joints. His inner thighs burned from the saddle, and the adrenaline that had spurred him to action began to flag.

He couldn't hear his feet hitting the ground but he could hear their horses' hooves grow louder. The tree line was too far away.

Then a harsher thought flashed through his mind: if he couldn't outrun them, he should surrender. After all, he wasn't permitted to kill any of them.

On the other hand, they had no right to kill or detain him either. No temporal power outside the church had any authority to do that. Who did they think they were?

None of that had any bearing on the distance to the tree line, or the acceleration of their steeds, closing the distance between them. If only he had reached the sea, he thought.

So he stopped. He clutched a handful of soil in his left hand, and then spun to face them in a crouched position, pressing his sword hilt against the gash on his left arm.

The riders pulled their horses wide, allowing the dismounted knights to rush him with their lances. They were taking no chances.

Elias feigned toward them, and then darted to one side, directing all his energy on the closest rider. He hurled dirt in the horse's face, and as it reared, Elias glanced aside the unbalanced rider's lance and drove his sword pummel into the rider's leg. Then as the rider pitched forward, Elias toppled, and replaced him on the saddle.

Elias swatted wildly at the incoming lances with his blade, and then spurred the fresh horse downhill toward the shore.

He tried to focus only on the animal's stride and the rhythm of her hooves, but he put little faith in outrunning a company of French horsemen who were rested and knew the town. Exhaustion was settling in, and his wounded arm burned, but something in him kept repeating: you must not be caught!

He thought about circling back toward the Templar fort by the harbor, but that seemed absurd. French soldiers possessed it completely.

So his only hope became holy ground. Sanctuary.

He rode through one church yard, without fortification. Though many graves lent concealment, this was no place to stop. These soldiers were too hot to be dissuaded by a frail gardener guarding a chapel door.

He scanned the tree tops for church spires. Something large.

He switched directions again, riding south down a lane until he spotted an abbey. It offered ten-foot high walls overgrown with foliage and fruit trees on the other side.

Elias rode alongside the abbey wall, pushed himself up to a crouching position, slapped the horse hard and then jumped.

He crashed through the foliage and landed with a thud in the orchard. He rolled back against the wall, pushed himself into a squat and clutched his bloody arm.

His mind raced. He didn't have long to make an appeal. And God preserve him if no one was home. While he might be able to hide until dark, he had few other options. After all, he just gave up a fresh horse.

His fears of isolation passed as he counted five serving women in the open grass. They stopped their tending and stared at him like cattle for several seconds.

Horses thundered past on the other side of the wall. Another moment ticked away in awkward silence as an elderly friar lumbered from around the side of the abbey with a maid at his heels.

The friar caught a look at Elias and his Templar vestment and whispered something to the maid, who scurried out of sight.

The friar approached calmly, his hands open to show he wanted to talk.

Elias pulled himself upright: "Praise God, Friar. Soldiers are out for me, in complete disregard for... I must request church sanctuary."

The friar stopped, momentarily lost for words, then held up a copy of the arrest order, "You, you cannot claim church sanctuary. The church is arresting you."

"It's not possible," Elias shot back.

The friar handed Elias the paper, "I'm afraid it's very possible. The charge is heresy."

Chancellor Nogaret gripped the lectern and gazed over the University of Cardinals, the honorable doctors and judicial scholars of the University of Paris. They were a noisy, skeptical bunch, and certainly wary of Guillaume de Nogaret, the excommunicate representing the French king.

"A bitter, lamentable thing," he began, reading his statement with as much emotion as he could muster, "Horrible to contemplate, terrible to hear of, a detestable crime, a thing almost inhuman!"

All mumbling ceased. Many who had witnessed the morning's assault on the Paris Temple glanced at Archbishop Sens for confirmation. He merely nodded, eyes downward.

Nogaret continued: "Indeed, set apart from all humanity, which now our King Philip the Fair has brought to light. In secret meetings the Templars denied Christ, demanded new knights to spit on the cross, and blaspheme the Holy One. Their leaders compelled them to kiss them... on the lips, then the belly... and other parts."

The murmuring began anew, rising throughout the chamber.

But Nogaret was not finished: "And from this ceremony of sacrilege and sodomy, they set to adoration of an idol!"

The room is in immediate uproar. "Among the Templars?" One shouted.

"It cannot be," sang another.

"If it could be proved," rang a third.

"The King requests," Nogaret pressed, "the use of the church's disciplinary power to compel the Templar order towards true confession."

Sodomy... Heresy... Idolatry... The friar read the arrest order aloud since Elias was no cleric, and couldn't read. But the words were so repugnant to him that they turned his stomach. His head swam at their implications. A few weak and overly-tempted serving brothers might fall prey into sin, but they had consciences. Besides, they had serving brothers, ministering priests, daily prayers, and confession. The holy sacraments! How could anyone think to accuse all of them?

Elias recoiled from the news, and as he did, noticed that the maid had silently ushered several French soldiers onto the grounds. They were heading for him.

The friar held onto Elias' arm, imploring him to closely examine the paper, but the friar's quick backward glance belied his intent.

"But we took vows to serve Christ!" Elias exclaimed, pulling free, "To protect people, feed the poor, to die for the cause of Christ as he had died for us. How could anyone call us heretics?"

"Brother, let us reason together," the friar followed, jogging after Elias, "Consider too those vows you made, to submit to authorities, your Christian brothers."

Elias sized up a fruit tree within an arm' length of the wall and began to climb.

"Brother, where would you run?" The friar continued, "Your order must submit themselves. Even now they're calling for crews to go after those ships."

Even now, the soldiers raced toward Elias, their swords unsheathed.

Elias scrambled up, snapping weaker branches as he ascended.

The Friar's words rang in his ears, "Return to your senses, brother! You're not at war!"

Elias spat back: "Come to your senses, friar! France has declared war on the Templars!"

"This was signed by the Holy Office!" The friar said, waving the paper at Elias as he leapt over the wall and out of sight: "Only the Pope can overturn them!"

CHAPTER 9

The patrolling guards at the Papal Residence in Poitiers opened the bed chamber door and glanced in, igniting a cross breeze from an open window at the far side of the room, filling the drapes like sails.

On his bed, a sickly Pope Clement coughed, "Close the window. I'm not well."

As one guard approached, a shadow moved behind the nearby chair. "A candle!" The guard barked as he drew his sword, and withdrew to defend the Pope.

Another guard entered, with both candle and sword ready. Pope Clement started up and squinted, "Who — who dares forfeit his soul by coming to kill me?"

From the shadows, Elias emerged, his beard cut, his Templar vestment gone. By all accounts, he looked like a common pirate. Sword in hand.

The Papal Guards raised their weapons and lowered their stances.

Elias took another step, and then with a careful nod, unwound the strip of linen cross-tied around his sword's hilt, stripped the splints and padding from its pommel, all to reveal its Templar symbol. He held it up like a cross as he knelt, "Your Grace, I've come to plead with you. On behalf of my Grand Master and all the other brothers. Why are you arresting the Templars?"

Pope Clement gaped, "I — I issued no arrest for the Templars!" He sucked in the air, and coughed, and coughed.

Moments later, Clement sat in a chair, sipping a broth, his hands shaky, reading the arrest order. Elias remained on his knees before him, with one eye on the two papal guards by the door.

After several moments, the Pope dropped the paper in his lap, "I didn't call for this. Indeed, it was for this very thing that I wanted a conference with your Grand Master. Before the rumors festered into something... And you. To be out of habit, out of protocol, absent the chain of command."

"The arrest –" Elias began.

"But you have superiors! Where is your marshal, your commander?"

Elias sighed. "I am a shipsman."

"You came like an Assassin," the Pope said.

Elias shook his head, "No. Assassins come like servants. That's why caliphs wear armor, even in the mosque." Elias made a stabbing motion to his ribs.

The Pope straightened: "And still so young. Well trained for one so young."

"Please, your Grace," Elias said, "You must overturn the arrest."

"Then I would be accused of heresy! We have procedures. Boundaries!" He coughed again and shook the arrest order at the window.

"Forgive me, your Grace."

"I cannot simply wave my hand and rescind such a thing. It is now a thing of record. Thousands must now be interviewed, by church commission. Evidence will be required. A general council must decide. The King himself must work through channels now, church channels. And the letter I shall write him will have fire!"

This, of course, sounded absurd to Elias. To imagine the Pope hiding behind some long-winded bureaucracy and correspondence when clear crimes had been committed in the name of the church. Then to consider that these councils might take years, Elias let the words escape: "While the Grand Master rots in prison?"

"Brother Elias," the Pope softened, "the church is God's hands on earth. We hold the keys of heaven, and for that, we are hemmed in on every side, by pagans and Mohammedans, by heretics and men who seek power. One rash command can spur a thousand revolts. Our response must be measured."

This was certainly true, and yet, "I thought," Elias sulked, "You could end this."

The Pope reached down and placed his hand on Elias' shoulder, "Think of my position. At this moment, I have only your word that these arrests are unjustified, only your naïve voice to plead the innocence of an entire religious order. This is not to say that your experience in La Rochelle does not have some merit..."

Elias' head began to shake in disapproval, as the Pope added:

"If you are innocent, then why were you sent to La Rochelle? Why did so many run, and with what, on those ships?"

Elias sighed, his eyes down.

The Pope held out his ring. As Elias kissed it, the Pope motioned to the guards, "See that he's well treated."

But before the guards could take a step, Elias sprung toward the window, "I was not sent out to be a heretic. You will have the proof of it."

The Papal guards ran to the window in time to see Elias descend to the ground on a rope, and disappear into the night.

CHAPTER 10

Then all the able men of France were on fire, kindled by rumors and stoked by great ambition to venture forth from their daily cares to port La Rochelle. For their sudden industry, their king would pay a king's ransom for those who fled on 18 Templar ships on Friday the 13th.

Every sea-worthy vessel stocked provisions and mended sails. Their newly signed crewmen, be they fishers, dock hands, or landlubbers, plied the local confessional for absolution, so that they might sail with clean souls. Their women lined the pews and prayed for security, good fortune, and for God's will to be done.

Their gossip of Templars as fat and lazy drunkards was exchanged for escapades of their fiendish devotion to discipline, skill and daring. To think, a secret group of their elite escaped the arrest, and absconded with untold artifacts from the Paris Temple! Surely the crew that finds them and binds them must be spotless and ready for anything.

And among these hopeful mercenaries, casting off lines and sharpening staves, Elias de Catalan worked with one eye fixed upon the horizon and the other on his sack of possessions, which included his map, sword, and his Templar vestment, tucked deep within.

The impatient pilot checked the wind and bellowed: "Cast off! Those Templars are days ahead of us!"

Elias helped secure the anchor. He sucked in the salt air, shifted his bulk to the waves beneath him, and felt strangely relieved to be back at sea.

Yet his present fortunes needled him. Had he obeyed the Grand Master in Paris, the woman Corinne might have died by a rogue's hands and he would have reached the ships, still ignorant of the arrest. Was that the peace Molay sought for him? And if Molay knew of the arrest and the dreaded charges that flew with it, why did he not go directly to the Pope and forestall all the followed?

It no longer mattered. Elias could not leave his innocent brothers to suffer wrong. So those ships must be found. Whatever the reason, they must return. Whatever was taken, it was not worth this terrible rebuke.

"No, they fled with the head of Sidon's demon lover, you ignorant sot!" One sailor disputed with another.

"Superstition," cried another deck hand, "They're monks of the Temple in Jerusalem. I bet 50 florins they carry the Holy Grail!"

"You're on!" Another answered, and side bets commenced.

Then they turned and bowed their heads as a skinny priest hoisted up an image of the Virgin Mary: "Oh Lord, in your mercy..."

"Hear you! You will soon be questioned," Chancellor Nogaret announced, entering the Bastille's prison chamber followed by several cowl-covered monks.

Molay emerged from the mass of now filthy knights: "On whose authority?"

"Yours is not the only office in direct authority of the Pope," Nogaret jeered.

A humorless priest for the Inquisition, Guillaume Robert, stepped forward, displaying his official seal against a small stack of ledgers.

"The Inquisition?" Molay exclaimed, half in disbelief.

Inquisitor Robert approached, "From these charges I have made a list of questions: one hundred and twenty six, to be administered with our chief witness."

Behind him stood the priest that confessed to Noffo in prison.

Molay shook his head in disgust: "I should have executed you, Florian."

By then, Florian's cell mate Noffo was busy searching the streets of Paris, examining every prostitute's face for his "Babylon," the loose-lipped Corinne. She knew something of the arrests. Perhaps she knew something else that might secure his fortune and put him in the company of the king.

Had he remembered the wound he gave her he might have saved his labor. The nuns and serving maids put Corinne to work serving other patients in the hospital. She nursed her own wound as well, and carefully flexed her arm, healing well.

The work was long but at least it kept her off the street.

Until the soldiers came.

Missing Templars were, of course, their reason for invading a woman's hospital, and they assured the mother superior they needed no escort. This excuse would not have held for long except that as they inspected the infirmary, a crouching nun appeared from among the large cupboards and darted for the exit.

A soldier snatched off her head covering, revealing a man beneath. They clipped his heels before he reached the first set of doors, and beat him into submission before he reached the open air.

He was no older than 30. A confession quickly followed, with assurances that he was no heretic but merely an accounting clerk from the Paris Temple.

As the soldiers congratulated themselves for flushing such an errant rogue from the shadows, Corinne draped a blanket over her arm, bore sufficient cleavage at the door to place herself above suspicion, then with a demure smile, stepped over the specks of the accountant's blood and snuck away.

She tried not to imagine what befell him, and all the other missing Templars of Paris. None but they could relate the actual interrogation, but many heard tales of what occurred in the bowels of the Bastille.

The poor clerk, without a moment of recovery from his recent beating, found himself hanged by *strappado*, his hands tied behind his back and hoisted up and dropped until his shoulders dislocated.

His screams harrowed the knights in the collective holding cell. They stung the Grand Master's ears as he sat in isolation, except for the rats that scurried over his bread.

The torture room became a single mechanism of forced confession, helmed by Inquisitor Robert and Florian.

"What happened in those secret meetings?" Florian demanded.

"The secret meetings," Inquisitor Robert volleyed, "We know you performed certain rites, but of what nature? Did you spit on the cross?"

Each Templar shook his head. The torturer then seared a burning iron against his victim's feet, convulsing him into a vessel of hot agony.

"You spat on the cross? You denied Christ?"

"More than once!" A Templar blurted out, begging them to stop.

But they did not stop. Templar after Templar endured the worst that the Inquisition could devise until they heard the most lurid tales any man might imagine.

"Was there a graveyard?"

Of course there was a graveyard, though they could not agree on where.

"And what did you see? Where was it? On top of what? A gravestone?"

Yes, a stone slab.

"A human skull?" Yes, but more. Much more.

A goat's head with horns? Yes, a goat's head with horns, but not only a goat's head with horns but the goat skull, but then it was a man wearing a goat skull with its skin still stretched over his features.

And the man? No one could identify him for he was wearing a goat's head! But he was naked, and he blasphemed the Holy One, or whatever phrase Florian and Inquisitor Robert agreed upon for that session.

One Templar said it was a demon. Another was not sure but after some motivation, and convulsion, concluded, "Yes, I killed God!"

In succeeding hours, the graveyard spectacle became in a dark, mystical ceremony. Blood covered a naked man wearing the goat's head, and he was spread upon an altar.

But the goat's head was brought in on a platter like the head of John the Baptist, but this too did not satisfy Inquisitor Robert, who asked if it had wings.

"Well, did it?"

Yes, wings large enough to suit the man! And this idol of the naked man with a goat's head rose up and demanded favors and offerings, mostly things for the benefit of a demon, the evil one Satan himself, and Sidon's demon lover, whoever she may be.

"What kind of favors?" Florian required. And again, ignorance and searing pain produced a wealth of knowledge...

"We kissed him wherever he asked!"

"Where?" Inquisitor Robert pressed, "On the neck? On the feet?"

The answers resembled questions and upon further questions, the answers came to resemble the charges Chancellor Nogaret specified.

"But what of its name?" Florian asked. The groans were unintelligible by the end of the week. "It was what? Baw – what? Baphomet? You said the idol's name! You said, Baphomet?"

"Please, please stop..." a Templar Standard Bearer cried, "Yes, Baphomet!"

And that name echoed through the dungeon to every man therein.

CHAPTER 11

With little luck, the sailors on the Bay of Biscay traded news from ship to ship:

Had they seen the Templar fleet?

South Hampton is clear?

Could 18 ships conceal itself upon the Irish coast?

What news from Paris?

Had they confessed?

Aye they had!

Would the devil give them safe passage if they sail off the edge of the world?

Knowledge of any kind could take whatever form it desired. Gaps in the tale might find a clearer shape after hours upon the watch.

And as the watch changed, the sailors told their tales: "Guard it well, the devil said, for it would be the giver of all good things. Then he gave the Templars... the ledger."

The other crewmen "Bahhed" at him like disbelieving sheep.

The Pilot, who stood most frequently upon the bridge, and so, perhaps had a better vantage to hear reports, joined the rumor mill with a firm: "Believe it. There were secret meetings. Believe there were unnatural things, as you have heard. But I didn't hear this from Paris. I heard from one who heard it from a prison cell in the South of France. It started in Aragon. A Templar priest killed his superior over it."

The crew cross themselves. God save them every one.

A priest in Aragon? Elias mused, leaning over the ship's map, his finger resting on that eastern region of Spain. The Templars were the front lines there against the Mohammedans. The Temple priests of Aragon must have borne many tales.

Out of habit he checked the wind and stars, and plotted their present course in his mind's eye, finding it off the English coast.

To confirm, he pulled from his garments his 8-point Italian compass, decorated with the fleur-de-lis at the North point (Tramontana), and a cross at the East point (Levante), to symbolize the center, Jerusalem.

"What's that?" One sailor said, squinting at it.

"A wind-rose," Elias answered absently.

"A compass," the pilot said, "Don't Templars call it a wind-rose?"

Several crewmen looked suspiciously at Elias.

"The better to hunt them by," Elias taunted, waving it at them and groaning like a ghost.

The crew laughed. The pilot smiled, keeping his eye on the strange man with the wind-rose by his map.

"They wouldn't risk the English coast," Elias said, half to divert them and half to prove he didn't belong among the rowers, "Not this time of year. If they didn't cut south... Northwest. There." Elias pointed.

The captain and pilot exchanged glances, glanced again at the map, at Elias, and then out toward the pale horizon.

In that same sky, hundreds of miles removed, an arrow plucked a goose from its soaring flock. Its brothers dared not break formation, and so the lone bird fell to the royal estate.

The next arrow missed the flock by a mile.

King Philip the Fair, a dandy even in the field, threw his bow at his servants for tarrying to fetch his fallen prey. He strode toward it while his court attendants moved in procession, with fans aloft to shield him from the unforgiving sun.

Other servants of the estate beat the nearby pond with large branches, driving the frogs below. Their croaking should not disturb the king's peace.

But his peace was not so easily won. The letter in his pocket seemed to burr him, and that was followed by Chancellor Nogaret, gingerly stepping over the field, trying to avoid the puddles.

King Philip drew him through the dankest patches and finally waved the letter at him, luring the chancellor ankle-deep into the mud.

"From his Holiness Pope Clement," the king bellowed, "An attack on the Templars is tantamount to an attack on the papacy?"

"My lord," Nogaret began.

"He says so! He questions not only the validity but the morality of your arrests, Chancellor!" And he began to read:

> "My dear son, we declare with sorrow that, in defiance of all rules, while we were far from you, you stretched forth your hand against the persons and goods

> of the Templars; you have gone so far as to cast them in prison and have not released them – the which causes us the greatest sorrow. It is even said that you have added to the affliction of captivity a further affliction which, for the churches' modesty and our own, we think best to pass over at present in silence…"

The King looked up, "A further affliction?"

"A holy persuasion, my lord," Nogaret answered, "For the heretics among them –"

King Philip cut him off, continuing to read:

> "You have committed these outrages against the persons and goods of men who are immediately subject to us and to the Roman Church. In this hasty action all men see, and not without reasonable cause, an insulting scorn of us and of the Roman Church."

"My lord –"

"He does not argue the innocence of the Templars, mind you, but the lack of respect for himself. For his office."

Nogaret stood his ground, "Then our reply must be that the knights will be promised pardon if they confess the truth and return to the faith of Holy Church. Otherwise let them be condemned to death."

"But if I am excommunicated, Chancellor, how shall you keep your head?"

Nogaret looked away, considering his words carefully. "My lord, such a day shall never come. But soon his holiness will, I believe, be persuaded not only to lift my excommunica–"

The king interrupted again: "He demands that we submit the Templars to a church commission immediately, which would remove the whole Templar order from your further afflictions."

Nogaret shook his head, and took a breath to slow the conversation. "That would be reasonable if we had all knowledge within our grasp. We would then yield them to his authority. But as it stands, some Templars escaped. Not just in Paris, but on 18 ships. We've sent our ships, and spies –"

"What if they are not found?" King Philip interjected, "If they're swallowed by the great ocean?"

"We still have such damning confessions –"

"But not from the Grand Master."

"No. I am waiting."

"For what? A miracle?"

"Yes," Nogaret said, smiling, "For Molay. We cannot risk losing him. His confession can tie everything together."

King Philip inhaled for another verbal jab but Nogaret continued: "Even if he just acknowledges this Baphomet, the whole Templar order becomes vulnerable, from the top down. We could compel the Pope to issue an arrest for all Templars, everywhere. Every castle seized, every treasury, opened. Think what that would do for your royal treasury. For your crusade to subdue Flanders. And others. I have delayed our interrogation of the Grand Master for this... Molay must be broken, but alive. "

King Philip mulled the words in his mouth, and then softened. "God's will be done. But do it quickly."

CHAPTER 12

Elias held a candle for the Pilot as they both examined the map, their compasses and the pitching waves. Through the darkness on the high seas, Elias pointed toward a faint fire signal. The Pilot steered, and motioned to crew to tighten the sail.

They had found the fleet. The Templar fleet! The sail and banners were unmistakable.

But there was more: they had gathered together with deeper, heavier, English cog ships, with higher gunwales.

"What in the name of —?" the Pilot began, and then seizing on it, "They're exchanging cargo."

Elias nodded, and made a quick assessment, "There's too many of them. We should signal them. Parley."

"No, we've got them!" the captain said, "Cover every lamp, and throw up the King's flag. We'll draw alongside and surprise them!"

Grand Master Molay winced at the candle rousing him from sleep. "Is it not still night?" He asked.

The guards ignored the question, led him down the passageways, and forced him to sit at a table. Molay turned, squinted at the nearby door, left ajar. He could see the shadow of the rack within, and glowing embers from the hearth. The torture room.

Molay could not see Inquisitor Robert but after a week of deprivation, he almost welcomed the coming footsteps.

"Is that you, Inquisitor?" Molay chuckled, calling down the corridor, "Dear Robert, has my turn come at last? You should have summoned me before my beard turned white. I might have kept you up week, and worn you out upon my bones. God knows my death shall only bring you disaster if you push too hard. And if you do not push, what will become of you when I report before the councils? When I, by God's provision, mount a just defense! God knows what rank deceits your fellow torturer bares. Esquiu de Florian infested many ears in Aragon. Now these deaths shall sure be on your head as well. Unless, sir, it is not yet too late to..."

Molay stopped. The footsteps came from Chancellor Nogaret, who strode into the candle light and set his pages on the table. He calmly sat opposite, his face as smooth as veneer disguising some grand, insidious device.

Molay looked away.

"We must talk, old man," Nogaret began.

Molay gathered his wits again, "Grand Master. And I'm still stronger than Pope Boniface when you came to visit him, excommunicate."

"We're both far from Anagni," Nogaret smiled.

He needed Molay to think so. This would not be Anagni for either of them.

That conflict involved King Philip seizing church tithes to directly fund his political Crusades. The two powers traded edicts until Boniface played an ace to trump the king. His Unam Sanctum declared all temporal powers were subject to the Roman pontiff to attain salvation. That is, if King Philip didn't follow orders, the Pope could simply bar him from confession, and therefore, heaven.

But the "greatest king in Christendom" could not be subject to the whims of what he considered a power-hungry Pope. So Nogaret employed his legal scholars to declare Boniface a heretic before the Unam Sanctum could be enacted. The charges ran with the familiar list of blasphemy, sodomy and heresy, but also included revealing the secrets of the confessional, stealing church property, the murder of Boniface's predecessor, Celestine V, and finally, secret sexual relations with a filthy demon that lived in a ring.

Nogaret could leave nothing to chance. Then he marshaled forces from Colona, and raided Pope Boniface's residence in Anagni, Italy in 1303. Soldiers crashed through its doors, scattering the servants and priests, with the battle cry, "Long live the King of France and Colona!"

As looting commenced, the elderly Pope Boniface scurried to his throne, quickly donning the ornamentations of his office.

Nogaret strode in, flanked by French and Italian mercenaries.

"Here is my head and neck!" Pope Boniface said, "The lawful pontiff and vicar of Christ, welcomes death for Christ's church!"

A moment after, Boniface was struck from his chair.

But as this raiding party turned to leave, they were confronted by thousands of Anagni townsfolk brandishing all manner of military and agricultural implements, together with chants of, "Release Pope

Boniface! Release the Pope!"

The mercenaries quickly relayed a message to Nogaret who was then cowering with his prisoner in the back of a hay cart: "Forget a trial in Paris! We must leave him if we're to escape with our lives!"

Though most would deny, some recall Nogaret saying, "Next time, I will choose the heretics!" before he struck the beaten Pope Boniface with his own hand.

Whatever the truth, Pope Boniface died three weeks later from his injuries. The hastily elected and decrepit Pope Benedict XI restored the peace by excommunicating Nogaret, and eventually forgiving King Philip the Fair while restoring "all graces" to Boniface.

"He opposed God and God judged him," Nogaret said, pouring a cup of wine, and setting it on the table before the Grand Master.

"He opposed the king stealing church funds for his private crusades, and he died from your cruelty!" Molay corrected.

"He set himself above the king."

"You will burn in hell for your king," Molay said, reaching for the cup.

Nogaret snatched it up and gulped it down. "Thirty six of your men have died already in questioning. Younger men. Stronger. And most have confessed to such horrible –"

"Get away from me, devil!"

"They said you were in those secret meetings, Grand Master. Are they liars? Shall I condemn them? Or you?"

"This is unlawful!" Molay started again.

"I am the law," Nogaret said, "And your confessor. Now I hold the sacraments you need to enter heaven."

If by heaven, Nogaret meant withholding access to Pope Clement, a lawyer, or a decent bed, he was right. Molay remembered Master Gerard's fears of what may become of them since Clement himself was at the king's mercy, but Nogaret was probably not able to pull those strings yet. Molay threw the jab again: "Strong words from an excommunicate."

"And you spat on the cross?" Nogaret returned without blinking, "In those meetings you denied Christ? Worshipped this idol? And what is this Baphomet?"

Molay's eyes widened. That word registered and he wasn't prepared for it. "Baphomet?"

Nogaret leaned forward, "What is its power that Gerard took it, and left the gold behind? What did it promise you? France or the church?"

Molay shrunk from the question as a man guilty.

Nogaret turned to a guard: "Get me some ink!" Then quickly shot back at Molay, "I can save you from the inquisitor –"

"I demand to see the Pope!" Molay countered.

"The last Grand Master of the Knights Templar should not die here! Like this? Think of your men. Very few confessed to sodomy, a private sin, with no proof –"

"I never!" Molay protested.

Nogaret slapped the document on the table, "Don't tell me; sign the confession. It will save you." His eyes shifted, as if the inquisitors were now stoking the irons through the nearby door.

Molay shook his head slowly, though his resolve was faltering. Was there anything to gain by signing a confession of heresy?

"It may even save others from being questioned," Nogaret continued, "We find more every day. Some hiding in cupboards, some disguised as women –"

"For the love of Christ!"

"Exactly! Embrace him. Sign, and the mercy of the church is yours, old man." Nogaret held the quill and plunged it into the jar of ink the guard set down.

Molay stared at the paper, at that cold line that demanded but a simple smudge from his old hand, and all his privations would end. He immediately felt the cruel pangs through his frame, the loss of sleep and food, the loss of fellowship and the light of day.

He thought of his men who still waited in filth, in a cruel queue that led only to the hot irons and *strappado*. He sent Master Gerard without him because he couldn't leave the innocent to suffer wrong. But they were suffering. And so was he. If one signature could end the torture, wouldn't it be a kind of unholy pride not to sign?

Then he thought that he might have the access he wanted: access to Pope Clement, access to resources for a defense, and out of Nogaret's hands. And he did not know what else Nogaret had planned if he still refused. The signature was all Nogaret wanted, and the Pope was still in the king's hands.

A distant groan emanated from the torture room making Molay wince again. Tears welled up in his eyes, "You heartless, villainous –"

Nogaret glared. "Sign, heretic, or be damned!"

No one knows how long the ensuing moments felt for this last Grand Master of the Knights Templar, but minutes later, Chancellor Nogaret sprinted from the Bastille, waving the paper at a government page waiting on horseback: "Take this to the king! Now we'll get the Pope to do his duty. We've got them!"

CHAPTER 13

A flicker reflecting on the dark ocean caught Master Gerard's eye. He turned a concave mirror against his nearest torch, casting light over the waves and upon the French ship.

"All Hands!" Gerard shouted at his crew organizing cargo. "Archers! Starboard side!"

Aboard the merchant ship, the Pilot threw off the covers to his torches. The king's soldiers warmed their grips, while deck hands checked the ropes and nervously bobbed their grappling hooks. They all visualized getting their hands on Templar cargo.

Still fearing the possibilities of fighting his brothers, Elias kept his back to the rest as he tied his scabbard to his waist.

Fire hit the mast!

The Templar ships lobbed a hundred flaming arrows at the merchant ship, sending them all ducking for cover.

The pilot attempted a change in course while the captain exclaimed, "They're attacking! Don't they see the king's flag?"

But it was too late. Unable to turn, the ship drifted alongside the English cog.

Elias quickly strapped his pack of possessions about him. He would leave nothing behind. He scrambled to the bow, and in front of the cowering deck hands, snatched up a grappling hook and hurled it toward the cog. He leapt straight after it, his hands full of rope. If the hook missed, he would probably drown, but at least that was better than being shot with flaming arrows!

The hook found its mark, and Elias scraped along the cog's hull. He clung to the rope for dear life, his feet scrambling for a hold. He found the coarse back of a barnacle and braced himself as waves crashing against his shoulders. His eyes closed as he did on his father's ship years ago.

He whispered a prayer, waited for the ship to rise on the wave, and then pulled hard and climbed up.

As he cleared the gunwale, the Templars lunged for him. Elias pushed off the side, and scrambled up to the poop deck, straight for Master Gerard.

Too concerned with the assault to heed a single assailant, Gerard stepped back as several sailors tackled Elias.

"Master Gerard! Stop your attack!"

Gerard spun, giving Elias his attention "Who are you?"

"Elias, Brother Elias! I come from the Pope!"

"The Grand Master's Elias? You brought this ship upon us?"

Elias yanked his head free to look Gerard in the face: "They've arrested us for heresy, a heresy they think you have! You must return to France… To prove our innocence!"

Gerard paused, and then turned back toward the assault: "Secure this man below."

They jerked Elias to his feet as he persisted: "You must! The Grand Master – "

Gerard cut him off, "I'm following the Grand Master's orders."

"No! You can't jeopardize all of us!"

"A sailor would understand," Gerard said, shaking his head.

"Are we heretics then? Are we?"

No answer followed as the crew dragged Elias toward the hold. He glanced toward the merchant ship, on fire. It veered away, like a large scrap of debris bobbing among the endless waves.

Elias went limp to force his body down. He re-centered his gravity, and snatched the nearest rope, hoping it would serve him, but it was long and loose, and produced no effect.

He tossed it in the air to draw his captor's eyes, and then he spun, head down, legs pumping to loosen their grip. He followed that by stomping his foot against the mast, propelling himself backward, and knocking everyone on their backs.

Elias rolled to his feet, slapped their hands away, scrambled across the deck, and with one terrible last look toward the merchant ship, plunged headlong again into the cold ocean.

CHAPTER 14

The following month beheld so many dejected vessels, none conveying any tale to compare to the one above. The returning commiserated the loss of time and the lack of clues to tie their promised fortunes to those 18 ships.

Alas the more, having then in hand so many damning confessions, even from the Grand Master himself, Pope Clement V reluctantly signed the largest papal bull from his office on November 22, 1307. In essence it read, "We have no alternative, but to request the arrest of all Templars, in every country, that they be held for questioning by church commission..."

England's King Edward II never believed the rumors and stalled the inquisition for as long as he could. When church emissaries and a Grand Inquisitor finally arrived like sullen tourists at the English Temple, they found only two elderly English knights guarding the vault. The Inquisitor berated the lone cleric with, "You don't know how many of your men are missing? You better have better accounting of your gold!"

They thrust open the vaults doors and their jaws drop. The room was empty!

Chancellor Nogaret shouted from the Parliament steps, "With a fleet of ships and English gold, the Templars only need men for an invasion now!" Then tossing another pouch of coins to his smug pirate Noffo, he ordered, "Go! Find something!"

No doubt Noffo expected a larger conversation, some wine, and perhaps that royal audience he craved, but not today.

Nogaret left his message ringing through the corridor as he plunged back into his office, and slammed the door. After a composing breath he said, "The king's best sailors all returned fruitless, not even a sighting, except for one piece of a ship with a few half-drowned mates... All who claim you found the Templar fleet."

Opposite Nogaret stood Elias, his jaw set and shoulders hunched, the posture of a man caught.

"Who are you?" Nogaret asked.

That was the one question Elias didn't want asked. To the ship's crew, his name didn't matter, nor would they have known its significance, but Elias was certain that the Chancellor was in possession of the staff ledgers, and the manifest from Molay's ship.

"One who could find them again," Elias replied, "If properly compensated."

"Another pirate?" Nogaret scoffed, "Some think you're a Templar on the run."

Elias noticed his hand rest on his sword. He could kill this excommunicate before he reached the door, possibly before he made a sound, but the Grand Master's rebuke and his ironic vows prevented him. Besides, Elias needed to find Molay, and Nogaret was the only path to that end.

"Many say you're devouring innocent monks for their money." Elias said.

Nogaret smiled, "Innocent?"

He held up a detailed drawing of a bare-chested man with a goat's head and horns, goat's feet, and large wings. A pentagram etched into its forehead.

"Recognize it?" Nogaret continued, "This is the idol they fled Paris with and attacked your shipmates to protect. Baphomet."

Elias drank in the picture with revulsion. "No man would ever admit to this."

"Really?" Nogaret taunted.

Within the hour, Elias was ushered past the Bastille guards, through the confusing levels and gates, and into a dungeon filled with tortured souls.

Elias could hardly look at them. Some faces he recognized, but they were shells of their former selves. They cowered before his gaze, ready to admit to anything set before them.

"We still don't know how far this heresy extends," Nogaret said, "Even the old Pope, Boniface, even he proved to be a heretic."

"I haven't heard that one," Elias said, struggling to maintain his wits.

"You spend little time in France," Nogaret said dismissively, "I told everyone."

"And all these confessed about this Baphomet?"

Nogaret nodded, and let Elias look around.

Still avoiding any direct looks, Elias scanned the group, "So which one is the Grand Master?"

Nogaret smiled, "Oh, we move him around in case some unknown Templars attempt something. You see, he burned his staff ledgers."

The embers in the Temple hearth ignited again in Elias' mind. On that night he should have fled Paris on that hay wagon, Molay had provided for his escape. There was no manifest, no ledger to accuse him. But Elias was still in the Bastille, and under scrutiny from more than just the prison guards.

"Well?" Nogaret said.

Inquisitor Robert offered Florian a closer examination of Elias' face.

Florian came within Elias' reach, and scanned his features as if inspecting fruit in a market, "I don't recognize him. Possibly."

"You're that priest that started this?" Elias ventured, a hint of malice escaping.

That was what Florian needed: "You Templars started this."

Inquisitor Robert waved his hand and the prison guards promptly braced Elias against a table. The Inquisitor grabbed a hot iron from the fire.

Nogaret strode up the steps toward the exit, "The Inquisitor is going to ask you several questions. You'll recognize them –"

"Wait!" Elias called.

"I've asked you two already." And Nogaret wasn't going to ask them again.

"You need me — I can find this Baphomet!"

"I employ too many pirates already."

"How many found the Templar fleet so far?"

"A Templar trying to reach his fleet?"

"How many know that drawing is either Egyptian or Persian?"

Nogaret's hand thrust out to stay the Inquisitor and his glowing iron. "How would you know that?"

"I'm Elias de Catalan. My father was Ramiro Moisés de Catalan."

"Captain de Catalan?" Nogaret said with emphasis, and perhaps a touch of admiration, "If that is so, why are you here and not hunting those —?"

"Because I found them," Elias said bitterly.

Nogaret descended the stairs again, "Found?" Nogaret repeated.

"In port. Off the coast of Acre."

"That's in enemy hands," Nogaret said, leading in closer.

Elias nodded, and Nogaret saw the satisfaction behind it: the young de Catalan had indeed found the Widow Peak and his pirate crew, and had his vengeance.

"If the Templars need men, they'll go to Aragon," Elias continued, glaring at Florian, "Aragon has the men."

The priest from Aragon flared his nostrils, drawing in an anxious breath.

"Well, Captain," Nogaret replied, "Then you'll need a ship. And proper compensation."

He waved the guards away. Elias straightened his clothes...

"You can't let this man go!" Florian bleated.

Nogaret ignored him and pulled Elias toward the stairs: "In Acre of all places. Well. You know, I lost my parents too. The church slaughtered them while putting down the Cathar heresy. Didn't matter that my father was not a Cathar." Nogaret glanced toward the Inquisitor, "Burned him alive. Not him, of course, but a man like him. But if it had not happened, I would not have gained my education in the church, my access to people like him."

"Yes," Elias said, not following.

"It isn't easy, separating. The pain — the rage — from the knowledge we must go on. To do our duty, eh? You want to be paid to find these ships, yes, but I cannot send misdirected rage. You have to understand, the Council of Vienne will convene in almost two years' time. Enough time for their inept commissions to interview and reexamine their confessions. It is also enough time for the Templars to do almost anything."

Elias nodded, trying to seem agreeable.

"You have a look of vengeance, Elias de Catalan," Nogaret said.

"I can separate."

"And I have leaks in security, so I must ask: where is your loyalty? To money alone? Glory? To vengeance again, if these Templars did something to you? Or as I believe, you have the strength and Godly character required to seek the truth."

Elias nodded, eyes flashing.

"Find this Baphomet, and I promise, the church will absolve you of whatever else you have 'found' in your life."

Nogaret directed Elias up the stairs and out under guard. Then he returned and glared at Florian: "Never question my strategies."

CHAPTER 15

Several hours later, a thin-faced spy named Jourdan ascended the Parliament stairs to the Chancellor's office. After bowing, he delivered the anticipated report on what the son of Ramiro Moises de Catalan did after his narrow escape from the Bastille: "Straight to the brothels, my lord. Pirates. Always a proper send off."

Nogaret paused and shook his head. "Brothels? No. Keep close. He's no pirate."

And yet, there in the brothels, among the drunken merriment and prostitutes, Elias roamed, looking over his shoulder for people like Jourdan, and actively pursuing a dark-haired beauty about so tall and possibly nursing a wounded arm.

He whispered in the ears of many girls along the wide road to his destruction, with many responding that Corinne was rubbish and they were better, as they pawed at him to further his investigation in their private rooms.

Elias refused, of course. Sometimes this caused a scene; after all, who was this determined youth to refuse?

But word got around, until one such woman of dubious repute, after pressing Elias for details he refused to give, stepped back through a curtain, and nudged Corinne.

As the matins in the Paris Cathedral commenced, a sleepy Elias sat, forcing his eyes to watch people go in and out of the confessional. Receiving communion. Leaving refreshed. The sweet sound of hymns beckoned him forward, but he had to shake himself. What could he say? Forget the comedy of roaming the brothels of Paris all night without tasting the fare. How could he unburden his soul and withhold his identity? He was wanted by the church!

"Forgive me, father, for I have sinned..." Elias might begin, his mind flashing to his fight with an Italian drunk, his threat to kill a king's chancellor before fleeing Paris, the melee in La Rochelle, his argument with a friar, his assault on the Pope's residence and all the other wayward thoughts and events he longed to dispel, and then slipping up just once and sprinting toward the door, the young priest yelling after: "Stop him; he's a Templar! Heretic!"

Elias rubbed his hands to keep them from shaking. He glanced at the soldiers milling about in the wings. They were there for only one purpose, he concluded.

A footstep clacked the floor behind him. Elias whirled, his knife stopping at Corinne's throat. Corinne mused, "Your kind is always trouble, sailor."

Elias pulled her to a dark corner, with her words trailing: "Are we finally running?"

"I'm not running; I'm hunting," Elias said, gripping her arm tight, "You have to tell me what's really afoot. You were close with Nogaret? One of his prostitutes?"

Corinne squinted, "You should take your slanders to confession." She clearly remembered every detail of their first meeting but Elias wasn't flattered. He glared until she began again, "I…" She stopped, deciding to play with the anxious fugitive, "No, I won't tell you."

"I'm not interested in you. You were Nogaret's leak in security, right?"

Corinne couldn't believe he was still so rude despite having scoured all of Paris for her. She glanced toward the nearby soldiers of the king, "It's better than beating the ponds."

Elias furrowed his brow.

"You know, on the estates. They make the peasants beat the ponds at night to silence the frogs. Not me, I –"

"Tell me about the heresy!" Elias snapped.

"There is no heresy. It's about money. You said you knew Nogaret..."

Corinne began, praising Elias' knowledge of the Chancellor's attack on the papacy, though that was known in all Christendom. What he failed to care about the another date, the one before Friday the 13th, when the magistrate broke the wax seal on an almost identical writ, "In the year of our Lord, July 12, 1306," she said, her tone biting, "Any Jew found outside our custody tomorrow will be executed. All possessions are now confiscate, and become the property of our King Philip the Fair."

She told him soldiers rounded up every Jewish man, woman and child, and shoved them about in the streets. Looted their houses. Those who put up a resistance or tried to run were put to the sword or shot down with arrows. She was lucky, perhaps, pretty enough to be overlooked among the prostitutes while her family disappeared.

So yes, she did live in the brothels, smiled and rode along in the official carriage to the Chancellor's bed. And there she learned that officially one hundred thousand Jews were expelled from France, under a single arrest. So yes, "When I saw those same sealed letters again on his desk, I decided to warn the frogs. And though I hate to admit it, it makes more sense now. Expelling the Jews was a trial run. No one would care about Jews dispelled. They really wanted to see if they could round up a whole population in a day. The king is really after your gold."

Elias pulled out the drawing of Baphomet: "Gerard left the gold in the vault."

Corinne stared at the drawing, speechless.

"You may not care, but if the king succeeds in condemning the Templars, no one is safe. You understand?"

"I've never seen this," Corinne said.

"What about a priest killing his superior, in Aragon? Florian."

Corinne again shook her head.

Elias stuffed the drawing in his coat again. He had already wasted too much time, and the woman was obviously a dead end.

As he turned to go, she held onto him: "I can help you. I can read and write –"

"If you had just beaten the ponds!" Elias said, pulling away.

"Before the Inquisition kills me, they will ask... about you."

Elias stopped short. Again, she was not his ministry, not his mission. But then he also deeply wondered: how long could such a lone soul survive? And could he trust her if he took her along? If they were caught?

Then again, a woman on his arm would dissolve all rumor of his affiliation with and allegiance to the Templars. Everyone knew that rule about women.

"Have you ever been on a ship before?" He asked.

After all, arrangements had been made. Elias held the captaincy of a small merchant ship with a singular purpose. His crew knew nothing but that they served under the direct command of King Philip the Fair, heading for Aragon.

Storms offered another destination. The winter winds streaked the deck as waves crashed over the ship's bow.

The Priest held up a placard of the Virgin Mary: "Oh Lord, in your mercy..."

Corinne clutched the gunwale and vomited her guts into the Atlantic. She did the same into the Mediterranean, her face shivering and wet with sea spray.

Elias pulled her up and tied her to the mast as he would any loose piece of cargo: "You're not much use. The crew thinks I should throw you overboard."

Actually the crew assumed she was his wife from all their bickering and hadn't said a word.

"Why can't you be kind to me?" Corinne whimpered.

The rebuke stung his resolve. He had been trained to be valiant in battle, and magnanimous to the nameless poor, but with her he had no guide. Had his decision to take her along saved them both or doomed them? He did not know. Ultimately, she was aboard his vessel, so her life was his responsibility.

He sighed against the storm, and then knelt and gently brushed her hair from her face. It was a slightest gesture, but it opened the portal of something he didn't dare express aloud: the truth was he did not trust himself. He wanted to be pure but not to be a prig. He longed to be noble, to save the order, to right the wrongs, to be the hands of God in the world. To fulfill his vows.

But with each punctuated moment the more he wanted to embrace her in the wet and warm her, to break his vows, and for her to prove herself as amorous as his thoughts and her reputation dared, for one night, one voyage, or for a whole lifetime, perhaps. But he was not free.

He pushed his feelings down as he stood, and patted the mast beside her, hoping to assure her safety if nothing else. Then he managed softly, "I hope you like Aragon, Corinne."

On the upper deck, Jourdan held his stomach too, and kept an eye on Elias.

CHAPTER 16

In a cold room of Chinon Prison, three French Cardinals sat beneath one small window and offered Grand Master Molay their full attention.

He hunched terribly with malnourishment, and conspicuously twisted his beard around his fingers as he said, "My confession was... I signed because I feared the torture."

"You mean your confession was a lie?" The first Cardinal replied.

Molay was slow to answer, "Yes."

"Then how can you help your defense?" The second Cardinal asked.

The first Cardinal continued, "You see, a general council must decide whether to suppress the Templar order."

"Suppress the order, entirely?" Molay said, eyes raised.

"If your men defy the council, they also face excommunication," the second Cardinal pressed, "Now, will you undertake their defense?"

"What a poor soul I would be not to! I will need lawyers... and money."

But in the same instant, the first Cardinal opened a ledger revealing the image of Baphomet. The demon with the goat's head flashed through Molay's mind again.

He looked down, and shivered. "I'm sorry. I can't."

The second Cardinal leaned in, "You can't? Did you say, you can't?"

Molay looked out the window and didn’t answer.

The third Cardinal straightened, "What just happened? Are you now refusing to defend your order?"

"If I could defend it in the open field!" Molay erupted, his hands gesturing widely as his body convulsed with emotion.

"What troubles you, Grand Master?" The first Cardinal asked.

"Is it the sin within you?" The second glared.

"I demand an audience with the Pope!" Molay blurted out.

"We have more questions," The second continued.

"My order was sanctioned by the papal office," Molay shot back, "Not Nogaret’s!"

There was a great pause, followed by, "How can we proceed?" The first Cardinal said, trying to settle the room.

But Molay only hid his face in his shaky hands, "May I have my priest, please? And the sacraments. The sacraments and hymns."

The Cardinals looked at him in disbelief, stunned at the change in the man who months before lead a grand procession of knights through the streets of Paris.

The second Cardinal relented, closing his ledgers, "Alright. It will be done."

On the shores of Aragon, Elias secured the vessel and directed his crew to unload the cargo. They were to trade its contents along the port so that by their industry their captain could move about without arousing suspicion.

Corinne sat on the dock, glad to be back on land.

Elias strode past her, nodding pleasantly that he had done his duty. He never asked for her feelings on anything but assumed she was satisfied to be out of France. That was, of course, her only request from their first meeting. And despite his passions, or perhaps because of them, he hoped his nod and subsequent head drop would be their last exchange. She was a distraction he could not afford.

He ascended the hill toward the Templar castle overlooking the shore. He found it deserted except for a few soldiers of Aragon, and his passenger Jourdan who tried to follow without Elias noticing.

The soldiers were quite accommodating, and assured Elias that he had nothing to fear, for they were standing watch. Their government had issued arrest orders as well, and armies marshalled against the Templars throughout the land. Most of the knights had been captured, and their possessions confiscated.

Some fled to the inland castles, to the front in the perpetual war with the Mohammadans. As one might expect, these hardened, disciplined Templars refused to surrender, and so, were besieged by their Christian brothers. How long that would last was uncertain but Temple Master Ramon Sa Guardia replied to messengers that after doing such great service for Christ, instead of confessing to evils they did not do, they'd rather die in their castle.

Elias thanked the soldiers for their diligence and sallied forth into the crowded market, with its many rows of produce carts. Elias kept Jourdan in sight and talked with various merchants.

The wood carver knew nothing of a murdering priest but confirmed that the inland Templars would rather die than confess to heresy.

A brewer snidely remarked that the charges must be true for what church or state would persecute the innocent?

The merchant by the vegetable cart scoffed, "Innocent? If they're innocent they'd have nothing left! The King's gobbled up all their gold, land, ships, everything."

By three o'clock, even the children in the streets were singing: "The Pope's in the pocket of the King, oh worthies..."

By then, Jourdan had grown suspicious of the many denizens who had more than a passing comment for Elias. He pulled something from his coat's breast pocket, and waved it at a few idle soldiers of Aragon, and then pointed in Elias' direction.

By then Elias also began to suspect that while Chancellor Nogaret bankrolled his freedom, he might wind up in the prisons of Aragon if he were not more careful.

That was when a peasant drinking by the brewer's cart introduced himself. The name was probably a lie and Elias quickly forgot it. But he could tell by the way the peasant stood, his hand heavy on the small blade dangling on his hip, that the man was used to a heavier weapon. He smiled at the children and after a few pleasantries, leaned toward Elias: "Priest, they say? Esquiu de Florian? He was the heretic."

"How do you mean?"

"He murdered a priest, didn't he?" The peasant gulped at his drink, "So he bought his freedom with the worst story he can think of about the Templars."

Corinne sidled up to Elias, "I found you a contact, a scribe."

"For the Templars?" The peasant sang out despite himself.

"Whores will say anything for a coin," Elias deflected, pulling

Corinne several steps away, "Stop risking yourself. I got you out of France, now –"

Elias sucked in a breath. Jourdan and several soldiers approached.

The peasant dropped his drink and took off running.

Where there's running, accusers chase. And as they came, Elias pulled Corinne in a different direction:

"Walk, 10 paces more, then run," he said. Elias ducked down and darted around a row of carts, circling back until he saw Jourdan again.

Jourdan kept Corinne in sight and swiveled his head around for Elias.

Elias drew his knife and crept up on him, counting steps: eight, nine...

Corinne took off. Jourdan sprang forward but in that instant he met with a flash of steel and a strong arm that sprawled him backward into a cart of melons.

The old melon merchant screamed at the confused spy, who scrambled to his feet to confront nothing but the angry merchant holding her broken produce.

He tried to placate her and reached for his inner pocket for funds only to discover it almost surgically slashed open and its contents gone!

Beneath another cart, and not so far away, Elias crouched, and examined his heist, which included an official Seal of the Inquisition.

CHAPTER 17

It was dark when Elias and Corinne approached a modest two story house on a quiet street. Corinne shrugged. Elias knocked.

A hunched Jewish man in his 50's, Simeon, cracked open the door. Elias held up the Inquisition Seal and demanded entrance.

Simeon squinted at the seal, "Sorry, my eyes are old. Virtus junxit?"

"No, Jew," Elias said, "A cobbler said you know something about the Templars."

"Sorry," Simeon said, and attempted to close the door. Elias pulled Simeon into the gap to prevent him as. Simeon squealed, "Let go! I don't know anything!"

"Virtus junxit?" Elias repeated, "I think I know him."

As Elias shoved his way in, hands grappled and wrenched him off his feet. Swords grazed their scabbards and flashed in the dim light.

"Wait!" Corinne lunged inside before the door slammed.

A group of four Templars of Aragon held Elias down while the former peasant from the brewer's cart uncovered a lamp.

"Virtus junxit, Mors non separabit," Elias blurted, "Whom virtue has united, death shall not separate. It's a Templar motto."

"Clever spy, are you?" someone said.

"I'm a Templar!" Elias returned.

And the men laughed. Elias still had the Inquisition Seal in his hand!

Corinne then turned and spoke to Simeon in Hebrew. And so, despite the argument and weapons and Elias' struggle on the floor, the language shift startled everyone still for several seconds as Simeon and Corinne conversed.

Finally, Simeon turned: "Let's hear them out, Commander. They're here about Baphomet."

At another quiet home, a cobbler's tapping ceased as soldiers broke in and surrounded him. Jourdan matched the cobbler's hammer with his dagger, and began a short interview that would certainly end with Simeon's address.

Meanwhile, Simeon compared the Baphomet drawing to several old texts. The aforementioned peasant, now an unnamed Templar Commander, paced authoritatively before Elias with annoyance, "Let it go. The Grand Master himself dismissed it as absurd. Here in Aragon."

"So you've heard of it," Elias said.

"I was there. Florian ranted about a secret society within the Templars," the Commander scoffed, using his hands to recreate the position of himself to Florian within the chambers of the Temple court, "Howling on about what another priest, his superior in fact, had received in the confessional. That villain had been pressing his ears to the wood, listening to the penitent whispers from sailors like yourself, on subjects it is certain that neither priest knew a thing about."

"He must have had some proof of —" Elias began.

"Suspicions, more like. Conjecture sprouting from the fertile soil of speculation. Much like your current... quest," the Commander spat, "Sown in idleness and gossip. We see full well the devilish ends he was carried to. He pressed his priest superior over it, like some grand and completely unsinewed conspiracy. He threatened to take it to the King of Aragon himself if he was not made privy to the secret order within the order. Sound familiar?"

The Commander pointed at the drawing of Baphomet, "He had his own version, though not so elaborate. His superior rightly demoted him... Though he never should have turned his back." and with that, the Commander pantomimed Florian striking down the superior priest with the nearby candle stick.

"'So your superior didn't tell you?' The Grand Master said. And there, Florian wagged his finger at his rude sketch and said, 'He said the knowledge would disrupt nations and many church beliefs!'"

"He said that?" Elias started.

"But the Grand Master said, 'But he never told you what it was." The Commander shifted position to imitate Florian:

"'I know you're stealing gold for the next Crusade for it! That I know!' Not a bad defense, actually, but the Grand Master was not distracted. He tore up the Baphomet sketch before his face and said, frankly with more composure than I would have, 'You killed an innocent priest, a brother in whom Christ dwelled. You should live a long time with that knowledge.' And that, Captain Elias, was the last we heard of Florian until recently. He was put in hard labor. He should have remained so. Though it is not our place to judge, is it?"

"So Florian didn't know, and Molay didn't tell you either?" Elias posed.

"It is not our place to question! The church will absolve us."

"Not as long as Baphomet –"

"It's nothing!" The Commander stomped, "A tall tale, compounded by greed, the King's greed. Is it not obvious?"

Simeon sets his hand on Corinne's arm: "Sure. Obvious. And we Jews were French once. All as clear as... As a banker's alphabet."

Simeon had an idea.

He bounded up and searched his bookshelf, rifling through volumes, "I must confess, your bankers give me a lot of work." Simeon plopped down a book on the table, opened it to a passage of tables, and began calculating letters on paper.

Elias glanced at the Commander, "What exactly does he do?"

Simeon popped up again, "It's another cipher. The Atbash cipher in fact."

Elias looked back without comprehending.

"It's Hebrew, word substitution," Simeon continued, "A equals Z, B equals Y and so on."

Elias started to catch on, "You mean you decipher our bank codes?"

Simeon smiled back and guided Elias' eyes to the paper:

BAPHOMET = [TAF] [MEM] [VAV] [PE] [BET]

"In Hebrew," Simeon said, "You read right to left. Baphomet..." Then he showed the line below:

[ALEF] [YUD] [PE] [VAV] [SHIN] = SOPHIA

"Sophia. Greek for wisdom."

If Simeon did not know Elias could not read before, he knew it now. Elias threw up his hands, "Huh? This is code for wisdom? What wisdom?"

"One you don't yet have?" Simeon said.

Everyone laughed but Elias: "If Baphomet is code, then it's real," he leveled, and a silence fell. Several Templars wrinkled their brows in thought.

"Don't you see?" Elias continued, "Florian didn't make this up. No one imagines a code like that. He stumbled onto something. Gerard fled Paris with something."

A torch light glimmered in the window.

The Templars rushed to investigate, and saw Jourdan, leading a troop of soldiers bearing torches.

The Commander blew out the nearest candle, "Good God, you led them right to us!"

Everyone filed through a back window. From the house, Jourdan blew a whistle, and the soldiers pursued them.

Corinne looked about and grabbed Elias' arm: "What about Simeon?"

Simeon wasn't with them.

"Commander!" Elias called, as he squinted into the shadows, and then rushed toward a nearby clump of trees.

The other Templars had since disappeared but the Commander tarried, his knife ready, to assure their escape. He was prepared to wound the careless renegade who jeopardized them, and leave him to the Inquisition, if necessary.

As Elias reached the tree line, the Commander shoved him back, "Isn't it enough that we survive? You're forcing the church to condemn us!"

"We're not going to be proven innocent by burying it all," Elias shot back, "Someone has to dig, Commander!"

The Commander wanted to dig out Elias' eyes, but he made no further advance. Elias seemed to plead for assistance with his hands open, but the Commander returned only a look of weary betrayal, followed by: "You're on your own."

And with that, he fled into the night.

CHAPTER 18

Four soldiers pulled a staggering Simeon by a rope that bound his hands. His mouth bled. His eyes barely open.

Jourdan secured the other end of the rope to a horse's saddle, and started their procession with torch in hand. As the horse lead, a soldier beat Simeon with a staff while others flanked him to make sure he stayed on the path.

The road divided at a hill running up toward the summit of the town. They took the lower road that lead toward the sea, or more precisely, toward the worst slums and the prison, where many a body are found and questions are not asked.

On the upper road, Elias pulled Corinne along, stalking them. Corinne averted her eyes — another Jew abused. But Elias held his gaze, gritting: "Never leave the innocent to suffer wrong."

He directed Corinne to ready a nearby horse cart, and then ran ahead of the procession to find his best advantage.

He considered his sword, a proper tool for cutting Simeon free, but not for rescuing him. Wrong as they were, Jourdan and the soldiers were Christians. Their lives could not be on his hands. But something had to be done, and quickly.

Elias saw a well near the wall ahead of him. It was low to the ground but its frame stood sturdy enough to secure livestock. So Elias drew up the bucket, counted rope yards for length, and then tied off the rope at the well's base.

Then he waited.

As Jourdan approached, Elias counted soldiers again: still four. The two on the sides had sheathed their weapons, and plodded along after the one in front who held the torch to guide them. The one with the staff lagged behind, his staff still prodding. He would have to be first.

Elias weighed the wooden bucket in his hand. It would be enough, he thought, but for what? A distraction? A rebuke? And how would such a rebuke be delivered against four of them, and the spy?

He adjusted his grip to several yards down the rope from the bucket, sucked in two quick breaths, and jumped.

Elias' knees plummeted into the soldier with the staff, crumpling him under his weight, and in the same motion, Elias pulled the bucket in, bashing Jourdan across the head.

Before the others knew what was happening, Elias batted away the torch. He kicked another soldier in the upper chest as he lunged back up the wall on the taut rope. A quick step, awkward to say the least, but with the torch down, no one could tell the difference. They knew only that their assailant was still in motion.

Before they could raise a torch for any use, Elias swung the bucket wildly, like a flail on a long handle, smashing anything that moved. One soldier fell before he could draw his sword. Another before he could duck. Jourdan took another blow to the shoulder that sent him sprawling.

Then in the dark, the remaining soldier – Elias couldn't tell which – found the staff, and whipped it blindly from left to right, managing to tangle up Elias' rope. As Elias pulled back, the soldier tackled him, grappling the rope around Elias' throat.

Elias tried to spin, to turn, but the soldier was strong and kept bearing down. He struck Elias with an elbow to the jaw, glanced off another blow above his brow, and then off balance, the weary Elias lost his handhold. The rope went under his chin and the soldier pulled back, choking off his supply of air.

As blackness began to envelope Elias' senses, the staff cracked over the soldier's head, lurching him forward. It struck him again at the base of his skull, and he slumped over.

Elias pushed him off. Simeon dropped to his knees beside him, his wrists still tied, his hands full of that splintered staff. They sat for several seconds, breathing. Elias sat up, and cut Simeon loose. They helped each other stand as Corinne pulled a big-eared burro dragging a produce cart toward them. They helped each other onto it with Simeon saying, "I've never seen a Templar do that!"

Elias held his rope-burned hands against his throat: "You're used to bankers."

And though Elias was perhaps too pained to notice in the dark, Corinne gazed upon him with such an affection that would worry him later. Every Christian she had ever known had either abused, condemned or dismissed her, including the Templar order she had helped, now more than once. But this sailor was different.

She whipped the burro and it managed a short, sufficient trot for their escape.

By dawn, Elias was bandaged and back on ship, directing his crew to cast off. He could not afford to stay an hour more. Jourdan would have his head once he or any of those soldiers woke from their infirmary.

On shore, Simeon walked in arm with Corinne saying, "You keep many secrets, Corinne, but I hear that you are not for boats. Why not stay here?"

Elias shouted from the deck, "Because she's stubborn!"

The shores of Aragon were no safer than France, she thought, and her face harder to hide in a coastal village than in Paris. The other reason she stored up as a secret for herself, though she allowed the quip to pass her lips: "He needs me." She followed that with a giggle, and hugged Simeon.

She climbed aboard with Simeon's words following, "But this journey may take you –"

"Anywhere," Elias finished. "Egypt, Jerusalem, isles covered with thieves and pirates, even remnants of the cult of Assassins. My father fought them for years. They will kill us if they catch us."

This itinerary was obviously meant to dissuade her. A few of his crew members lost all complexion but Corinne met Elias' gaze, softly determined to go along.

Elias relented, trying to ignore his discomfort for the moment while addressing Simeon: "Keep deciphering. Find out what you can. And pray that we find this 'wisdom' before the Council of Vienne."

"To find ships that do not want to be found? It will take a lot of prayer." And Simeon opened his arms toward the blue Mediterranean, dotted with ships out unto its vast horizon.

CHAPTER 19

The vast sea swallows two whole years of our story then, dawning over a busy Syrian port. From a minaret, a muezzin called the town's inhabitants to Morning Prayer.

On the sandy streets, our Florentine pirate Noffo, his head covered and face partly obscured in a white keffiyeh scarf, motioned to two Assassins to follow. That is to say, they were not simply killers. They were adherents of the cult of Assassins, dedicated to the cause of Nizari, and the slaughter of their enemies, which included Templars.

The three began to follow someone: a tall, lanky gentleman, also in Arab garb, who deliberately walked in the shadows of the main street, not just to avoid the cruel morning sun, but to avoid being seen from the nearby mosque.

Viewed from the sea, they might look like a small parade, though its leader was unaware. He stopped, perhaps too long, admiring two European ships at port.

Then the man turned down a side street, and upon passing a dark corner came into the path of a dagger held to his gut. The man stiffened, but then quickly grinned and said, "Here to lose your head, Brother Elias?"

A similarly dressed Elias emerged from the shadows and withdrew the knife, "Still such a diplomat, Raymond."

They embraced and laughed like old friends, then shushed themselves, and whispered for several moments before heedlessly walking together toward the mosque by the sea.

"The caliph wanted me for his French ambassador but I begged him for Germany instead," Raymond said. "They haven't arrested their Templars yet."

"Still so cheerful," Elias responded, almost with a sigh.

"At least I don't work for Nogaret," Raymond nudged.

Elias nodded, "You're the only Templar who will talk to me now." News of his so-called betrayal in Aragon had fallen hard on his ambition to restore the order.

"Beware the eighth deadly sin, brother. Sadness. Calls our gracious God a liar."

"Do we not have reasons?"

Raymond smiled, and walked on. More than once he almost spoke but Elias kicked a rock or glanced out at the ocean. Raymond finally summoned his resolve and took Elias' arm, "When you get tired of reasons, I know a little village north of Tunis..."

Elias resisted, musing how diplomats always have something on the side, but Raymond held on, "Listen, I'm serious. Tunis, along the coast. Every year in August –"

"Are you asking me to renounce the faith?" Elias interrupted, "Abandon my brothers? And the Grand Master?"

"No. it's –" Raymond stopped himself this time. He glanced up then restarted: "You know, I often pray Gerard bought us a country with that English treasury. Not that they have enough for all that, but –"

"I know," Elias said sadly. "Look, did you find what I –"

"In the mosque." Raymond plodded forward. "If there is a Baphomet in the world… A cleric, keeps a lot of those old scrolls Saladin took from us in Jerusalem."

"Can we trust him?"

Raymond shook his head no. "The better question is: what will you do then if you discover –?"

"I don't know." Elias patted his friend's arm, knowing they had to part, and quickly. There was no use tripping over the unspoken. If Baphomet was real, the Templars and their Grand Master really had received the promise of some satanic horror in those secret ceremonies. Then how would that knowledge fare against their souls? And could Elias really hand the damning proof to Chancellor Nogaret?

Raymond began to lure Elias away from the mosque, down another street toward the market, but Elias stood firm: "You could come with me."

"No, I... Besides, if you're going back to France..." Raymond held his hands up in playful surrender. They nodded to each other for good luck, and then Raymond disappeared among the worshippers exiting the mosque.

And Elias went in.

Raymond kept his head down, split off from the crowd as they reached to the first carts at the market. He trusted Elias would find the cleric without difficulty, and if his bribe was sufficient, he would be ushered into the records room.

Perhaps it was the thought of Elias' potential discovery that quickened Raymond's steps. Or his second guessing. He had set up the meeting so easily, established through the caliph's diplomatic contacts. The document samples from Alexandria seemed genuine enough. Perhaps he shouldn't consider it too closely, he thought. Things like that just happened.

But something still gnawed at him. It was inexplicable but he found himself making one right turn, then another, seeking a shortcut back the mosque, to that dusty records room on the other side of several bookcases where the Cleric laid out hieroglyphic scrolls before Elias:

"Why do you seek this, infidel? It’s heresy. Won’t help."

"Won’t help me what?" Elias returned dismissively.

The Cleric shrugged and opened his ledgers and scrolls like a merchant selling silk in the market. Among the texts were many faded drawings, some like the ones on Elias' map, others like the angelic drawings he knew from the Templar chapel in Cyrus. Then his eyes fell upon the image of a goat-headed man examining stars. Baphomet himself. The strange lines, jutting from points off the page, pulled Elias deeper into the text.

"The Ptolemies, from Alexandria," the Cleric said. "They were star gazers, mathematicians. Heretics. They believed in a round world."

Elias sets his jaw. "A round world? Next you’ll tell me the sun doesn’t rise or set."

The door creaked on the other side of the bookcases. Elias glanced up briefly but saw nothing. His mind conjured thoughts of Raymond coming to stop him. More than anything he wished Raymond had come so he could share what he was seeing, to get some confirmation or denial of what the scrolls meant.

But Raymond was on the narrow street, and alone until he passed another dark doorway, where he came into the path of another curved dagger held to his gut.

This time he snatched up the Assassin's wrist as it slashed through his clothing. He felt the warm pinch into his flesh, probably a shallow cut, but Raymond was too busy to check. He tangled up his assailant, drew his own dagger, and lashed out, blade on blade in the doorway.

Both sliced and parried as Raymond retreated, feigning back to draw his attacker forward. Then Raymond stomped hard on the Assassin's ankle, toppling him back into the shadows.

Raymond charged up the street as fast as his legs could carry him. A few steps were all he had before a keffiyeh scarf engulfed his head. Noffo pulled him back into a doorway and plunged his sword through the threads. The white scarf turned red, and the renegade diplomat sank down without a sound.

"No sanctuary, Templar!" Noffo jeered, "Tell me who’s in the mosque and I’ll spare his life."

Without a moment's breath, as Raymond convulsed, Noffo inspected his victim, tearing his clothes and emptying pockets, "Come, confess to me, Templar. Who is he?"

From Raymond's belt, Noffo pulled two gold coins with the English insignia. He held them before his victim's dimming eyes, as if demanding an explanation. Noffo almost regretted stabbing so deeply into so deep a well of information, but the man was still his enemy and Nogaret's heretic.

Alas, he was also dead.

Noffo kicked him to make sure, and then raced toward the mosque, abandoning both his victim and the lame Assassin groaning in the gutter.

So close was he to discovering the secret of the missing Templar ships! The English coins were no coincidence. Raymond must have known. The man in the mosque might well know as well. If only Noffo could reach him before he's dispatched by his other friend, the other cautious Assassin, who had creaked the door open and slowly drifted behind the stacks of religious literature.

And Elias, heedless of the danger, only felt the weight of his own burden, his hands full of ledgers. Others would have to decipher the drawings and text. His mind ran to France, perhaps to the dark prison cell where he might accuse and demand the answers from Grand Master Molay himself. Had he really sold their souls for this heretical Baphomet?

Elias glanced at the patient cleric who offered no expression that might reveal the Assassin as he took his final steps toward his goal.

Elias turned too late. The Assassin's dagger slashed Elias' chest, the same way Elias slashed Nogaret's spy in Aragon, the same way he demonstrated before the Pope.

The ledgers crash to the floor. The cleric cheered, "Kill him, he's a Templar!"

The Assassin drove Elias backward, but only enough to clear the fallen ledgers. Then Elias shifted his weight, spun the Assassin toward the wall, and kicked the Cleric from his path.

The Templar grappled with the Assassin as he tossed the dagger from hand to hand, slashing Elias' torso. Finally as they pressed teeth to teeth against the tables, the Assassin pulled Elias' tunic open to reveal chain-mail armor underneath.

"I know you Assassins too!" Elias spat, pulling his tunic over the dagger, and yanking him into the Cleric. And as they tumbled, Elias drew his sword.

Noffo couldn't see the blood splattering over the ledgers, but from the door of the records room he could hear grunts, gnashing teeth spitting profanities, crashing furniture, and the steady pulse of a sword in terrible industry.

Noffo stared at the door and listened, his own sword ready. He waited another moment, attending the silence. Then he cursed under his breath. His prey was waiting for him.

He kicked the door open and flashed his blade through the gap for good measure. Seeing no resistance, he plunged inside.

He darted through the passage of book cases and came to the tables covered with blood, the floor covered with blood, and the cleric's body standing, pressed against the wall.

Noffo's head moved on a swivel, left to right, as his blade flashed up and down around the edges of the book cases, searching for his dangerous suspect.

He listened and came to realize only the sound of his own breathing. His eyes settled on the cleric, finally noticing the long red scarf that kept his body erect, trailed up and out the broken window above his head.

CHAPTER 20

Elias dropped a tunic full of ledgers on the shore, and plunged his bloody, shaky hands into the sea. He scrubbed up to his elbows, and waved his bloody sword back and forth in the surf, before dropping his whole being down.

Then for a briefest moment he was seven again, clinging for life to his father's ship, praying for the strength to hold on, and not to drown. He heard the call of Molay to let go. Hugh Von Grumbach calling him the "Little Assassin" and how he owed his life to the next Grand Master of the Knights Templar.

But before he dared to dream of such a fellowship, the boy had to let go. So he pulled himself up the rope and over that gunwale. Only he was twenty, and the ship was not his father Ramiro's.

T'was a bright moon over the port of Acre and Elias had covered himself in pitch. Once on deck he hurled a torch onto their resting sails. The sleepy crew had but a moment to stir before Elias smashed a gourd of liquor against the mast. Flames splattered across the deck, lapping up the planks, the ropes, the sails.

The pirates shouted expletives as they scrambled for buckets, and threw water at the blaze. A few just ran, colliding into one another and clutching their best belongings before lunging into the sea.

Those that sought Elias discovered that he had exchanged his arson for slaughter, mercilessly dispatching all comers with sword and dagger.

Then aft, by the light of the mast, Elias found his prime target shouting for his ship's deliverance, and for justice. Perhaps the captain with the widow's peak should have cried for something else. His aging sword drew fast enough, and wagged as well as it had before, but it lacked substance against the advancing pirate lad entering his prime.

Elias parried away the scimitar with ease, and ran his own blade up to the hilt into the captain's ribs. He gasped, rendering up from death a look of curious disbelief. Who was this youth that he would dare such an enemy shore, so scandalous a ship, so dangerous a foe? Whose child was he that he could do this?

That curious but hopeless expression was almost identical to the one the Assassin gave in the mosque records room, as he struggled to untangle himself from the cleric, his eyes caught in the glint of Elias' armor.

Elias hacked the Assassin's blade away, along with the hand that held it. A quick and terrible inspection of two men's entrails soon followed, while they slipped on their own blood, seeking cover.

Then the Templar stopped. His frame seized against his pulsing veins, holding firm until he could see what he had done.

To take it in. To file it away. To justify it.

The moment stuck, unwilling to pass.

Elias could not recall how he bound the ledgers and scrolls, or by what sense he knew the window was his only escape, or how he knew the cleric's keffiyeh scarf was long and strong enough.

He only knew as he came gasping, shaking from the surf that he was loose on an enemy shore and in sight of his ship!

He wrung out his tunic, scooped up the ledgers, and strode toward the port while forcing his body to seem relaxed. He struggled vainly to control of his breathing, and then belted out louder than he meant to: "Cast off! Immediately!"

He rushed on board, surprising both his crew and that of the neighboring vessel.

A genial captain from Sicily stood calmly on deck, still hoping to finalize a sale:

"Ah, you're back," he said, motioning to his barrels, "You like the olive oil, eh?"

With the beating drum of time in his head, and the growing expectation of well-armed killers rushing toward him from the mosque, Elias nodded absently at the barrels and then began kicking his crew into action.

He muttered toward the Sicilian: "Can't say if it's pure. It's Italian."

The Sicilian replied, almost embracing Elias, "If a sailor can't recognize a virgin, he's been at sea too long!"

Both crews laughed, but the Sicilian held his joke for the woman's response.

Corinne had tried to remain inconspicuous, but with her sea legs established and two years of confident purpose in her windswept hair, she had become a gross distraction for all the men.

For the last hour, she managed to deflect most of the Sicilian's teasing by talking with an elderly chaplain who had wandered aboard. But with Elias raging and a decision on the barrels to be made, Corinne surprised the lustful Sicilian by taking up the matter herself. She tossed him a pouch of coins and said: "God grant us all a fair delivery..." Her mind danced for something clever that wasn't too sexual, "And a, such a gracious inspection. We'll haggle with you another time."

The Sicilian sniffed pouch of coins as if it were a love token, curtsied and kissed her hand.

Corinne withdrew before he could attempt anything further. Her attention remained with the chaplain. The man seemed eager to speak with Elias. Corinne seemed eager that they should meet, but Elias brushed them off, avoiding eye contact: "Be quick with your blessings, father. And be off."

"Elias, he's brought news," Corinne said, "He's waited –"

"No new passengers!" Elias shot back, his hand on his sword as a threat. "Cast off now!"

His crew quickened in their duties and the Sicilian elegantly withdrew, tossing both the pouch of coins and another joke to his crew.

The disappointed chaplain lingered in disbelief for several uncomfortable seconds. Corinne apologized, almost at the point of tears, and then ushered him away.

Elias stormed into his cabin, dispatched the ledgers, and then personally assisted the crew in weighing anchor and setting sail.

The vessel obeyed, leaving port as a tardy Noffo ran along its planks in vain to catch it.

CHAPTER 21

In cabin, Elias transferred the stack of ledgers to the table. His arms thudded down their tension momentarily. He shut his eyes and willed his thoughts toward the bright horizon, full sails and that inner tempest safely stowed.

Next to him, his nautical map lay silent, almost withered from use. Lines crossed from port to port, all over the Mediterranean and North Atlantic. He had been everywhere.

Corinne entered, waving letters: "Elias, he's a priest! He waited a month to give us news from Aragon!"

She then noticed the ledgers oozing blood and water on the table. As Elias huffed, and tore off his tunic, he noticed them too. He flung the ledges into the corner.

"What did you do, Elias?" Corinne asked.

"Not now. Get out." Elias peeled off his chain mail shirt, revealing a slight wound and bruised ribs.

"My God, Elias." She reached to help him, but Elias cut her off:

"I told you — I'm hunting. You're no help to me now."

Corinne silently explored Elias' troubled face but refused to move.

Elias swallowed and said through gritted teeth "Baphomet refers to the Ptolemies. Killed a thousand years ago, for heresy. Can't tell Nogaret that, can I?"

Corinne held up the chaplain's letters again, "A defense is growing. Many have revoked their confessions. Even Florian had to ask the King of Aragon for money."

Elias slapped them from her hands. "None of that matters if we're guilty."

Corinne threw her arms around him. Elias fought the urge, before succumbing to a deep, passionate kiss. Moments passed as they rested comfortably in each other's arms.

"Your heart is pounding."

"I can't. I can't."

"Why? Why couldn't God call you for something else?"

Elias pulled away: "Sweet Jesus, I'm a Templar knight!"

Corinne sighed, launching into the same argument they must have had a hundred times since Aragon: "God made you Elias Ramirez de Catalan."

"I am the Grand Master's Captain and a Templar! If I'm not, then I'm just... another… pirate."

That was new to Corinne. All the other episodes had ended in a recitation of the order's codes, the temptation of women, or the gallant hope of restoring the order's glory. Sometimes all of the above. Sometimes all that preceded them making love.

But this time something else shook loose and both of them knew it required more than his sullen silence. Elias' eyes danced about, unable to settle on the intimacy in front of him: "Sure, my father really did kill those Assassins, helped gain peace with Antioch. The truth is, he didn't know the Sultan was on the ship. He was looting it. It was a miracle."

Corinne did not know the private history of Elias' father, nor was she sure if he was kidding but she couldn't help but laugh.

Elias smirked, then kicked the sack of ledgers, "Maybe it's a question of which lie you can live with. But I can't just go off to... Rendezvous in Tunis! Or like you. You'd rather be a French whore than –"

Corinne stopped his mouth with another kiss. "Don't you think I..." She pressed her warm hand to his cheek, "I run to keep us from Nogaret. From being like him. Oh, I could get close enough, like this. Close enough to poison him. And myself. But I wasn't made for that. And the Grand Master sent you out –"

"So I wouldn't kill him!" Elias finished, pulling away again: "If this is heresy, why didn't Molay execute Florian in Aragon? Let me kill Nogaret in Paris?"

Corinne shot back, "So it isn't heresy! So it is heresy! Maybe it was a conspiracy from the start and the Pope absolves you anyway! The world may never know, but you still act like this is your only hope."

She knew she had pushed him too hard but she wasn't sorry. She wanted to understand this terrible loss of honor or salvation that continued to spur their expedition. Only if he could confess and unburden himself of whatever was standing between them.

Elias crossed the room and put on a clean shirt, leaving Corinne standing alone. He hunched over the table again, glaring at his map.

His evasions could not continue. Corinne knew it. She sucked in her bottom lip, summoning her resolve: "And what happens if you succeed, love? How will you explain me to every crew?"

Had Elias felt the full impact of the question he would have dropped into a chair, but his finger was tracing the space between Aragon and France.

"Elias, didn't you hear what I said?" She asked.

Perhaps Elias had but he ignored her still. He scooped up the letters and pressed them back into her hands: "You said Florian wrote the King of Aragon for money?"

"Yes."

"Florian was imprisoned in Aragon. So how could he make his confession in Toulouse, France?"

Corinne shrugged, not following.

Elias turned and snatched up the sack of ledgers, "I've been chasing the wrong lie."

"What are you doing? Elias?"

Elias heaved the ancient ledgers and scrolls of the Ptolemies out of a nearest portal into the Mediterranean. Then he nodded to Corinne: "Read Florian's letter."

Corinne focused on the window, her eyes wide: "Elias... "

"The Templars are revoking their confessions. And they'll never prove us guilty — not if I can ruin Nogaret first. Read the letter."

"My Lord, remember what you have promised, that if the deeds of the Templars were found to be evident, you would give to me 1,000 pounds in rent and 3,000 pounds in money from their goods..."

Elias let the words ruminate and spur his journey's end, to Paris.

The government offices buzzed with industry. Rows of scribes composed stacks of pamphlets saying:

"Corrupt Pope Defends Heretic Templars"

"Prison Confession Reveals Pope As Satan's Pawn."

Various lords mingled like so many pigeons, pecking for whatever might profit them in coin or absolution while Florian strutted about, bowing to whomever seemed important, assuring each: "The Templar defense is not much. All denial without proof."

And into this corrupting stew Elias strode in, and proffered a letter to the nearest guard: "Go tell Chancellor Nogaret his prosecution of the Templars is over. Go now."

And in his thoughts, still the words of Florian flowed: "...And now that it is verified and when there is a place, think fit to remember."

Remember, yes, the promised thousands of pounds in rents and goods — this Elias mulled while finding entrance to the Chamber of Propaganda. Florian looked up but before the former priest could place the face, Elias' backhand sprawled him: "There is your payment, knave!"

The scribes and lords scattered. Florian scurried under the tables, and Elias overturned them in turn, pamphlets flying. He grabbed Florian and pounded him again, "You never knew anything, did you?"

The accusation carried through the chambers to the Chancellor's office.

Imagine for the economy of time, that at that instant, Nogaret was in conference with Noffo, also having just arrived. He bestowed upon the Chancellor the two English coins, and expounded on the violence in Tunis, and of the suspicious pirate now thundering down the hall.

The Guard entered, greeting Norgaret with Elias' letter in hand, while down the hall, Elias kicked Florian into a ball, and heaved him like a sack of refuse over another table. Then he climbed over him and began to strangle: "You never saw the rituals! The sodomy! Where did you first hear about the Baphomet? In prison? In Paris?"

Florian shook his head but after more choking, he nodded.

"In Paris? When you tortured those men."

Florian nodded, weakly.

At last, truth is in the air, Elias thought. Though any reasonable man might have reservations about such a coerced confession, Elias didn't care. He flung Florian toward the door, and Florian ran out, still gagging on Elias' final words: "You'll never be safe, villain!"

The humiliated former priest rushed past the lords and the pages, past the guards, even past Nogaret and Noffo. Noffo smirked, ready for his turn in the Chamber of Propaganda, but Nogaret held him out of sight, and sent in the guards.

As they converged, Elias countered, hurling stacks of pamphlets, and then wielding a chair to protect himself.

The Chancellor entered casually: "Captain Elias, I thought you may have been eaten by cannibals and antipodes by now. Or have you eaten all of them?"

Elias held out the paper: "You wanted the truth? Here's another copy of a letter sent to the King of Aragon."

"That was not your mission."

"My mission keeps coming back to Florian," Elias pointed.

"I sent you after the Templars!" Nogaret stomped despite himself.

"No, you sent me after Baphomet." Elias signaled for the Chancellor to clear the room but Nogaret did not budge. The guards were staying.

Elias set down the chair: "A church in Aragon will confirm this tale, as I have heard. It's about an avaricious priest arguing with his superior, the one who actually heard confessions from visiting Templars. You see, Florian never knew anything about those secret meetings. Had no understanding of any secret rites, but his suspicions were base, so vile that his superior meant to put him out. But Florian struck first. He killed his superior, and was sentenced to a life in prison.

"But he gained the opportunity to write a letter, and slip a coin to the jailer. Since he had nothing to lose, he wrote the King of Aragon, trading charges of heresy within the Templar order for his freedom, and then some. The King must have agreed, but didn't follow through..."

Elias flung the letter at Nogaret, "So he sent a letter to you."

Nogaret let the paper fall, "You have no your proof of –"

"The truth," Elias interrupted, "Just ran out of here! How else could Florian get to Toulouse prison? You moved him, to give you a confession and a witness on French soil. That was the excuse you needed to arrest the Templars. You set them up."

Nogaret motioned and the Guards grabbed Elias by the arms.

"Copies of this are all over!" Elias bellowed, pushing against the Guards and grasping the table to secure himself: "Your prosecution is crumbling! Your only hope now is to condemn Florian, and release the Templars! It's over!"

The two stared like challengers in the field until the Chancellor smiled, "How much did they pay you, Elias?"

"If the Templars are found innocent, the church will condemn us to hell."

"Is that why you punished Florian?"

"He's a murderer and a liar."

"So are you, Elias," Nogaret said, and the words stung. But Nogaret would not suffer him to the tortures of the Bastille. He tossed up some pamphlets, like confetti at a royal party, goading the ambitious son of Ramiro Moises de Catalan. "The truth always needs some persuasion.

Promotion. How else do you think crusades get started?"

He let that hang in the air, and then: "Yes, I used Florian to expedite our cause, but I was certain of the Templars' guilt years ago."

"Based on what?" Elias spat back.

"That's why I need you to find Baphomet."

After what Elias just did to Florian, after the evidence presented, Elias gaped that Nogaret had no intention of backing down. Had he heard nothing? Was he actually sending Elias back into the world's void in search of damning evidence?

"We're out of time!" Elias said, wrestling for his wits, and certainly unable and unwilling to present the discarded ledgers of the Ptolemies, "Only the German commission is left, then the Council of Vienne."

"The Pope gave the Templars more time."

"And your prosecution grows weaker with every confession they revoke."

Nogaret leaned in, "My dear pirate, do you know what happens to heretics who revoke their confessions?"

CHAPTER 22

On the 11th day of May, in the year of our Lord, 1310, a row of cardinals sat in the Council of Sens and listened as knight after knight confessed to having confessed because of the torture.

None of this came as any surprise to Nogaret, who hosted Elias in the wings, positioning his guest as close as possible to the proceeding.

Elias, on the other hand, wanted to hide away lest any recognition place them all in further jeopardy. And yet, he had to maintain his role as a dispassionate, truth-seeking mercenary if he had any hope of helping them.

He barely breathed through the council's interview with the Paris Sergeant, the man that stole the staff ledgers for Molay, and ordered the young, stubborn sailor to abandon the whore for La Rochelle.

In tears and with a fragile lilt, the Sergeant recounted, "I know nothing of Baphomet. I would have confessed to anything to make them stop."

"Then why the secret meetings?" said someone from the tables.

"Foolishness?" He shrugged, and reached down to scratch his leg: missing. His limbs were stumps burned up to the mid shin.

The interview lasted for more than an hour before Nogaret signaled toward the Cardinal's table, and then whispered to Elias: "We've heard this for months. One after another."

The Archbishop Sens responded to his queue, slamming his hand down: "Enough! I cannot abide this further. As dogs return to their vomit and fools to their folly, so the heretic relapses into error and denial. God is not mocked."

He stood and closed his ledger. The Cardinals, startled but not surprised, stood and withdrew, as guards picked up the Sergeant and carted him from the room.

In total there were 54 Templar knights in the following procession that led from the Council of Sens out to the carts, which were then drawn outside the walls of Paris to a field between St. Antoine's and the windmill.

And in that field stood several rows of stakes, 54 in all, each surrounded by piles of kindling.

And to each a Templar prisoner was tied.

The Archbishop Sens gave the homily for all who persisted in their innocence, the sum of which might be expressed as: "Relapsed heretics, persisting in your sin, you fall outside God's mercy and must therefore be destroyed, to burn in eternal fires prepared for the devil, his angels and all who abandon the truth."

The guards lit the kindling. And there, before many pious onlookers and convinced functionaries, Elias walked with Nogaret, powerless, as his brothers burned.

Their final screams entered his Elias' ears like daggers.

Somewhere along the row, and certainly while bending Elias' attention, Nogaret tossed Florian's letter into the lapping pyres: "Now the Pope will have to grant them time to rebuild a defense. God willing, that should give you the time you need."

The Chancellor may have patted Elias' shoulder along with some assurance, may have offered other inspirations, threats or promises. The Templar heard none, but with a hard nod, his quest reinstated, walked toward the city depths with tears streaming down his face.

He even failed to notice the narrow-faced spy, Jourdan, trading information with Noffo by St. Antoine's. The approaching Chancellor grinned with satisfaction, and then handed the two gold coins back to Noffo and motioned for him to follow Elias.

In a prison known only to a few, the jailer delivered the fate of the 54 defenders to their Grand Master, along with a plate of vegetables. Molay failed to understand at first, then dashed the plate aside: "Please, send word, again. The Pope must grant me an audience."

The jailer replied, "Would you hang the hopes of the Templars on a man who keeps confessing and revoking? You're lucky to be alive. Sir."

CHAPTER 23

For two days Corinne had rolled her hands in vivid expectation, infatuated with the dream of Elias' fatal blow to the king's cruel crusade, and of her life thereafter. Could the son of Ramiro Moises de Catalan truly abandon her and return to his pious disciplines? Or would he demand some special dispensation, or seek an annulment from his vows altogether and take her forever as his mate upon the sea?

Two days had passed since he left. She could not fathom why there were no parades by now, no joy in the streets, as sanity must reign again upon the earth.

She heard the latch, and sped toward the door to find the most dejected man ever to enter a brothel. His flushed face told her everything, though Elias stood briefly trying.

Then he moved past her, and piled his necessities into a bag. She softly approached him but neither spoke for several minutes until he said: "The German commission opens in four days. I have to find someone."

Corinne tried to throw her arms around him but he pushed her off: "The Council of Vienne. Only Vienne."

Nothing else mattered. The world remained in that terrible intermission, the age between Friday the 13th and the Council of Vienne, when her love, as the "Hands of God in the world" had to toil. To Elias it was a curse that could be broken only by the truth behind Baphomet. Whatever it was, or represented to the Templar fleet, it had to be dragged back to Paris and laid at the Chancellor's feet. Or until the Pope regained his authority and absolved them.

There were no other doors save one, and it led to Germany. Elias left without another word, and rode faster than his horse had to La Rochelle, faster than his cart back to Paris.

In under three days' time, as dusk led many to their repose at a German Templar Fortress, a knock called the porter to open the door a crack...

Elias slammed through, charging across the room. Fifteen German Templars erupted from their dinner, drawing swords, as Elias bounded over the long tables to the chamber door at the far end of the room...

He slammed his shoulder into it, breaking it open. And there before the hearth, Elias found the man he sought.

A chubby Archbishop of Metz banged the official seal to start the German Commission, on the 14th day of May in the Year of Our Lord, 1310. Unlike the extravagant French, the Germans began rather sleepily, with their Bishops nodding and exchanging pleasantries with one another before taking their appropriate seats. Across from them a row of Templar clerics, seated like accountants, nodded with equal civility and waited for their queue.

The Archbishop began, "All those representing the Templar order..."

That was perhaps as far as the Archbishop got before a ruckus commenced in the anteroom. At first it sounded like a crashing of a great shelf full of books, echoing through their vast chamber.

No doubt the Bishops bristled and requested that their pages cease whatever it was.

But before anyone could respond, they found the chamber doors splayed wide as Hugh von Grumbach, together with 20 fellow knights, advance up the aisle to the commission tables in full armor and on horseback, flags waving from the end of their spears.

"Who is it that calls us heretics and sodomites!" Hugh thundered, "Bring forth these accusers and the judgment shall be rendered by God on the field of honor."

Hugh's opening profoundly altered the tenor of the proceeding. And with such proximity to the tables, and thus having achieved their full attention, Hugh continued, proclaiming the imprisoned Grand Master Molay to be a man of deep faith and personal honor and that he and the Templar order were innocent of all charges.

He compounded his assertions with an assault on the French Pope, saying Clement was a completely evil man, and hereby declared him to be deposed because he had been unlawfully elected.

Then, bending low to meet each council member's eye, Hugh reiterated their innocence, and that all knights present were prepared to risk their temporal lives in personal "trial by combat" with their accusers, to let God decide the issue.

The world did not have to wait long the German council's decision. It took but a few days before the news reached Paris, where Nogaret slammed his books against the shelves, papers flying: "Innocent?"

The Archbishop Sens nodded, gazing at his feet, "The German Bishops were unanimous."

"Damn all you pompous cowards!" the Chancellor stormed. How could the Germans fail? All the French Templars who had retracted their confessions embraced them again under the light and heat of 54 immolated knights. There should be no more consideration other than the divestiture of assets.

"You will receive papers from me before morning!" Nogaret continued, thudding down several heavy tomes onto his desk and rifling through the pages.

"On what subject this time?" the Archbishop immediately wished he hadn't asked.

"The Denunciation of Pope Boniface," Nogaret flashed, "Before Vienne I will have his heretical bones dug up and burned! And Pope Clement with them if he stands in my way!"

While the Archbishop no doubt pondered the relevance of this new device in the Chancellor's mind, in Metz, the German Templars laughed heartily, and ate heartily in the open air, and shared their table with all the poor.

Hugh slapped Elias on the back and escorted him to a chair, "I tell you, I do not believe in Baphomet. The Grand Master is as good a Christian as ever a man could be good. We will tell them so again at Vienne."

His confidence was infectious but Elias still held to his mission, "Someone must know."

Hugh said, "If Molay wanted to keep a secret –"

"A secret that sails off, steals treasuries, eludes capture? For what? And here you are, doing God's work as if your future doesn't depend upon this."

Hugh dismissed the thought as it were a fly, followed by: "I heard something… About an ambassador for the caliph, found dead in Syria."

Elias started up. Hugh pulled from his pocket two gold coins and placed them in Elias' hand, "He sailed from Genoa. A lot of English gold is now circulating in Genoa."

Elias gaped at the coins for several seconds, muttering, "Raymond lied. He knew... Genoa?" And the answer came like a shot: "Ships. They're building Italian ships."

Hugh shrugged, "I heard this from an Italian. You'll like him - he's a pirate too."

Then Hugh motioned to a man across the room.

"Can you scrounge me a crew?" Elias said excitedly.

"How far are you going?"

Elias smiled, recalling Raymond's words: "Tunis."

And through the crowd the man emerged... Noffo.

CHAPTER 24

"You know, in Tunis they hang pirates," Elias said, scrutinized Noffo, not able to place him.

Noffo smirked, "And behead Templars. Which you prefer?"

Elias replied by placing his hand on his sword, which made Noffo smile.

They couldn't decide if they worked best together or apart, but they tried both while trolling the towns both north and south of Tunis. They bartered what they could, inquired about the caliph's diplomats, set traps of opportunity, even flashed the English coins on occasion, but several weeks of toil led to nothing or to a brawl.

Both preferred the simplicity and anonymity of the sea, so they settled into a watch. The small Templar crew busied themselves, tacking back and forth along the coast, while Elias and Noffo cataloged the vessels, mostly small boats with lateen sails.

Noffo squinted at the two quick Roman-looking ships with square masts, but soon dismissed them. They were the same merchant ships they inspected a week before.

"What will you do when you find Baphomet?" Noffo began the conversation again.

"You mean the head of Sidon's demon lover?" Elias teased, "The Holy Grail?"

"I followed the money, not the rumors. Whatever, they will not give it to you."

"You didn't have to come along," Elias said.

"I say this because..." Noffo paused, trying to find the words. He liked Elias, and like Elias, he seemed familiar but he couldn't quite place the face: "Your loyalty must break somewhere. These men did not rescue you, little Assassin."

"Hugh has a big mouth."

"Big heart too," Noffo said. "Many nice heretics in the world. So what will you do? Kill them?"

Elias shrugged, his hand upturned from his sword, "You think Nogaret will absolve me if I do? And it turns out they're innocent?"

Noffo laughed. That was an absurdity he had never considered, though Elias wasn't sure which was funnier: that the Templars might be innocent, or that absolution was even an option — for either of them. Especially if Nogaret held the keys of heaven.

Both of them knew their salvation would come like a siege, not bestowed but taken by force. Their fulfillment would be as simple and as impossible as proving someone else's condemnation.

For Elias, those men were his brothers in arms. Worse, after so many years, he felt that he had joined the order to serve a God that abandoned him. God had certainly abandoned the Grand Master, and that dampened the certainty of every fugitive. The order was guilty of something. Elias just didn't want to go to hell for it.

And then, there it was, as Elias looked out among the other vessels. He grabbed the ship's rudder and came about: "That one. The one with three masts!"

At the time there was no word for a Carrack. The ship wasn't much larger than the others, but it had a deep draught, two square sails and a lateen mizzen sail — the first of its kind. What other glory might the builders of Genoa build with so much English gold?

Elias followed the Carrack along the coast for miles, until the sun set.

The Carrack anchored, and Elias drifted past in the dark, his crew prone in dead silence. Noffo plumbed the shallows with a pole while from the Carrack a small boat rowed to shore, lit by a single lamp.

Elias motioned to the crew, and they climbed into the water. Noffo grabbed his arm: "Ready to face Sidon's demon?"

"Stay with the boat if you want." Elias said, and Noffo plunged in right after him.

Through the darkness, Elias, Noffo and the crew crept through reeds and sand, and into a forest of tall oaks. They weighed their steps and tried to keep branches from whipping their faces or cracking under their feet while following the lamp, and an unknown number of Carrack crew.

The rows of oaks abruptly ended at the perimeter of a grave yard. Elias and Noffo held for a time while a couple of Carrack crew continued on with the lamp. Four or five others fanned out behind them among the row of gravestones. Still more remained at the tree line, also fanning out to encompass the area.

"They'll be on top of us in a minute," Noffo whispered.

Elias scurried behind the first gravestone and then motioned to the others to continue to flank right. Noffo dove forward, keeping up with Elias.

A Carrack guard strode up right next to Elias, and seemed to look into his face. Elias remained as still as the stones, breathless.

Noffo put one hand on his sword, but finally the guard continued past.

Then into the lamp light came to a few others from an opposite direction. This was not to be a burial but a meeting. Beside a tall gravestone, the lamp was raised, and Commander Gerard's face glistened as he held out a ledger: "Guard it well, for it will be the giver of all good things."

This must have been either coded language or a joke, but whatever it was, Noffo and Elias exchanged glances with Noffo heaving: "That's it."

Another Carrack guard appeared above Noffo. Noffo reacted, clutched the man's scabbard before he could draw his sword. The guard yelled instinctively, and Elias leapt up and socked him in the jaw.

Everyone turned toward them, with Gerard bellowing, "Report!"

Elias turned toward the woods, lying: "Soldiers advance!"

The Carrack crew charged Elias while Gerard grabbed the ledger and ran for the woods.

Elias' crew leapt up to defend themselves while Noffo and Elias darted around gravestones, avoiding the attackers.

Elias flew after Gerard, with Noffo lagging behind to protect their back.

Through the darkness Elias followed the sound of feet rustling through leaves.

The rustling stopped. Elias stopped and listened.

The rustling started again. Elias stepped onward, and called out, "Gerard."

Several more seconds passed, pursuing. Elias' percussive heart and breaths consumed all else. He slowed to a stop, barely able to see anything. No sound.

Leaves rustled nearby…

Elias reacted, sword up, and clashed — Sword on sword, teeth to teeth. Gerard drove Elias back with all his might, with Elias barking: "Gerard, stop! It's Elias!"

Elias turned, disengaged, and crossed swords again. And as they tied up and Gerard reached for Elias' grip, Elias snatched the ledger from Gerard's cloak.

They wrestled over it with their free hands, swords still entangled until Elias pulled free. Gerard's sword swung wide, clipping a tree just as Noffo swung around it and stabbed Gerard in the ribs.

Gerard groaned and fell to his knees.

Elias howled, waving his sword where Gerard's might have been had it stayed in his hands, his mind pleading for a different outcome.

"He might have killed you," Noffo's words rang in his ears.

"Are there more?" Elias spat back, sending Noffo's focus back toward the graveyard.

Elias stepped on Gerard's sword and embraced him, whispering: "Gerard, it's Elias. Molay's Elias."

"Don't give it to them..." He groaned.

Noffo motioned to Elias: "Come on! Others are coming!"

But Elias was ever closer to the fallen captain: "What is it? What does Baphomet mean?"

"A sailor would understand." And Gerard's breathing ceased.

The forest thronged with many feet. Noffo pulled Elias up, and with a last look back, they charged away blindly, branches lashing them.

As they reached the water line with their ship in sight, Elias dropped to his knees, and held up the ledger to the moonlight, reflected on the water.

He squinted at page upon page of coarse encoded text, intermixed with gruesome drawings of skulls, stars, and fantastic animals.

"Oh God!"

Noffo crossed himself: "The devil's work!"

"Oh God!" Elias repeated as Noffo pulled Elias into the water:

"Come, it's worth a fortune in France!"

CHAPTER 25

People of all tongues and stations flocked in the October air of Vienne in the Year of Our Lord 1311, for what every soul truly proclaimed to be the trial of the millennium.

Elias and Noffo observed the faces as they passed through crowds and caravans and improvised markets on their way toward the Council. Noffo began to sing excitedly despite himself, and quickened his pace. He was to be paid, and promoted, and become as a king himself among the minstrels and revelers. The end of his mission could not come soon enough.

In such anticipation and rapture, Noffo failed to see Corinne cross in the opposite direction, glancing but not drawing attention. He pressed on, and finally turned to find Elias gone.

In a little row house, Corinne entered, lingering at the door, and leaving it ajar behind her. Elias glanced over his shoulder, and entered after her. Then unseen they rushed into an embrace and kissed until they needed breath. They studied each other's face and sighed to control their tears.

"I was so worried," She said, "You little Assassin."

"Little… Is he here?"

Corinne nodded, "He's been waiting for you for days."

After a prolonged gaze, she led him toward a side room warmed by a hearth. After a meal long with stories, Hugh, Elias and Corinne sat with the Baphomet ledger.

Hugh refused to touch it but nodded softly and every few seconds blurted out, "Burn it."

"If I do that," said Elias, "I'm calling the Grand Master a heretic."

"Elias, you'll never prove this isn't heretical," Hugh insisted, tossing up his hands. "And you should know, the Pope lifted Nogaret's excommunication."

"What?" Corinne exclaimed.

"To stop his constant attacks on the papacy. Now everyone is afraid," Hugh said, and nodding again at the ledger: "Burn it."

Elias imagined himself standing with Molay before that hearth in Paris, what burning the staff ledgers had meant for his escape. He also remembered all that he shoved through that portal and into the sea, all the deception that had gone terribly wrong, and the punishing year apart from the ones he loved. No, he would not burn it.

He shook his head and Hugh nodded with disappointment.

"What do you intend to do?" Elias asked.

Hugh crossed himself with his thumb, kissed it, and laid his hand on Elias' head: "Stay clear of the proceeding. We cannot risk our most valuable spy."

Elias shook his head again. He couldn't do that either.

And so, in short time, within the great chamber, the galleries filled from the outer doors to the Papal throne. Thousands stood outside while church officials entered, and Noffo paced in the wings, searching.

Elias entered cautiously, and as Noffo quickly closed the distance between them, Elias filed through the gallery, straight to a center table where Nogaret was cheerfully sorting his papers.

"Where's the ledger?" the Chancellor began.

"Safe," Elias responded, feeling Noffo's blade against his kidneys.

"This is no time to haggle," Nogaret said, looking up.

"Look, Templars have many codes, ciphers –"

"Give it to him," Noffo growled.

"I will," Elias said, his eyes still on Nogaret, "If you drop your prosecution."

Nogaret started, "You're mad!"

"You kicked your way back into heaven, now let them go. They could be innocent."

Nogaret waved his hand toward the Papal throne, "If they're innocent we'll be condemned for attacking a sacred order! They have to be guilty!"

Too loud. The church council turned. Nogaret bowed at them until they looked away, and then gritted his teeth at Elias, "Don't you see? We must strike now. The church is weak, blown around by opinion, by pressure –"

"Yours!" Elias spat back.

"And with less defiant popes, we'll make more secure treaties. We'll bring our provinces into line..."

"Condemn to hell anyone who disagrees with –"

"We'll have peace, Elias! Our kingdom has a thousand hard choices to make but not this one. The Templars stopped the Mohammedans. They served their purpose."

"The Templars serve God, not you."

Nogaret raised his brows, "The king must have no rival."

Before Elias could reply, their attentions were at once arrested by the growing commotion in the galleries. Like a wave, the people rose and murmured as guards led a sullen procession of Templar prisoners to their seats. Some in the galleries hissed, some jeered, but they all fell silent as there entered one at the rear, with white hair and hunched shoulders, and flanked by guards.

Elias' heart leapt, but his frame refused to budge. He steadied himself against the table, and waited for their eyes to meet. But the Grand Master they led to a prime seat in the defendants section was not the Jacque de Molay Elias recognized. He didn't defy the council or even the accusing peasants with so much as an upturned head, but like an ancient, with frail features and a lost countenance, sat and stared at nothing.

Nogaret leaned toward Elias: "Stand with us or die with them."

Trumpets blew, startling Elias again. King Philip entered with his attendants. Then Pope Clement shuffled in, and slowly climbed to the Papal throne above the row of Cardinals.

Elias had to act, and quickly. He shoved Noffo back, and glared at Nogaret: "You are full of words. You wouldn't risk your most valuable spy."

And on those words, Noffo's mind raced back to Paris, to the whore by the chapel and that phrase from the young arrogant: "You… You are a Templar."

The chamber doors then sprung wide as they had in Germany. Hugh entered with his entourage of knights on horseback, calling, "We stand to defend the order!"

But they were not in Germany. The French King's guards barred them with spears and swords.

Elias rushed toward the Pope: "Let them be heard!"

Nogaret also rushed into the aisle and proclaimed, "These Templars are enemies of the church, come to overthrow our sacred justice!"

As the Guards attempted to dismount the German knights, Hugh spurred forward, "We stand to defend the honor of our order, and we have two thousand knights outside the city, standing by!"

King Philip stood, his knees shuddering, "Two thousand?"

The thought pierced every soul within the chamber: had the religious order the king sought to destroy surrounded the city?

Nogaret whirled back to Elias: "Do they?"

Elias glared back, "Let. Them. Go."

And despite the crowd and the great influence of the mounted knights, Elias felt the eyes of the Grand Master upon him. As he turned, Molay's frame sank further in disbelief, his lips shaping Elias' name.

But Elias would not let any disapproval melt him again. He set his jaw, almost defiantly, and addressed the Pope again: "Let them be heard, your Holiness!"

Nogaret's admonition followed, "Your Holiness, they threaten to overthrow the church! Arrest them, now!"

Pope Clement squinted at Elias, at Nogaret, back to Elias and Molay, and from him to Hugh and the soldiers and the knights...

He rose, his hand quivering, and addressed Hugh: "Withdraw your men. The council is suspended until further notice."

Moments later in the garden walkways, King Philip withdrew, his officials scurrying after him, and Chancellor Nogaret lunging to catch up: "My lord, it's a trick! They couldn't possibly... "

King Philip turned and struck Nogaret, and the procession halted for an instant. Nogaret swallowed the shame, his eyes downward, his cheek reddening.

The King then directed his other officials: "Send for my armies, immediately!"

Across the garden, guards whisked Molay onto a wagon, and though Elias pushed through the crowd, he could only watch as he disappeared from view.

Within the hour, in the woods outside Vienne, lines of mounted Templars slowly turned. In desperation, Elias repeatedly hacked a tree with his sword to punctuate his language as Hugh calmly secured his saddle, and said:

"They will not hear us. So, we have no choice but to withdraw."

"No," Elias railed, "We stay until we are heard! If we don't stop them now –"

"No Templar," Hugh interrupted, "shall ever ride into battle against the church."

"We did not stop the Mohammedans from conquering Europe so that these men could lord over us! We defend the innocent!"

"We will not kill our Christian brothers."

"If they will not hear –"

"They are not ready to hear!" Hugh thundered, "And we shall still not become their enemy."

"You're condemning us all," Elias said, his voice pleading, "Were you lying? Have you not enough knights?"

But Elias was wasting his words, and possibly his good repute. Hugh could not abide that. He mounted up, and while his favorite Assassin stood hopeless and dejected, Hugh said, "My dear brother Elias, our hope is in God. What else can we do?"

And thus, the Poor Knights of the Temple's melancholy, uncounted cavalry disappeared into the forests beyond Vienne.

CHAPTER 26

On the 22nd day of March in the Year of Our Lord 1312, as thousands of the King's soldiers surrounding the council chambers, Pope Clement read his bull, "Vox in Excelsis," which in part related:

"With intervention of our dear son in Christ, Philip, the illustrious king of France, we have proceeded, through long review and interview. But we could not remove the scandal of the Templars..."

Grand Master Molay sat silent, bewildered by the words…

"Other important orders have been suppressed for lesser offenses without fault to their brethren. Therefore, with a sad heart, by apostolic provision, we suppress the order, and its rule, habit and name. We forbid anyone from now on to enter the order, or receive or wear its habit, or presume to behave as a Templar. If anyone acts otherwise, he incurs automatic excommunication."

In the town of Vienne, Corinne held onto her crushed Elias. For her, though Clement's bull was not their chosen path, she saw its wisdom: the immediate peace. No more inquisitions, no more trials, no hanging condemnation.

She held and shushed and consoled Elias with the notion that he could resume the identity he had forged before his vows, "You did everything a man could. You weren't condemned. You're free!"

"To do what?" Elias replied, "To bow to this lie, that king. Submission is not peace."

"We could get away, be married," she said. Wasn't that obvious?

But Elias looked at the entrance to the row house, its door smashed open, its room ransacked. He muttered, "Nogaret won't make it that easy."

Elias ran to a loose stone at the base of the hearth, reached into the cracks and pulled out the Baphomet ledger. He had to verify its safety, but in so doing, he only put it back in harm's way. Two French soldiers along with Inquisitor Robert had watched from the adjoining room.

"By order of the church, you will be questioned about certain docu –"

That was as far as the Inquisitor got before Elias pounced. He struck the Inquisitor directly, and then beat the two soldiers with the surrounding furniture until they were down.

Corinne pulled at Elias to run but he brushed her off. He dragged Robert back into the side room: "Now I have questions!"

As the door slammed against her, Corinne pounded and protested, "Elias! Elias, don't!" But he was beyond hearing, and in the brief moments that followed, she heard the crash of wood and steel within.

Then screams.

She cupped her ears as the cries increased, until she could bear no more.

She grabbed her outer garment and fled the house. She did not know where to go but the road was full of departing folk, bored with the church council and eager to trade their anecdotes of the past several years of hunts and trials.

Corinne joined the festive caravan, and made fast friends to ensure her escape. She forced a smooth front and an attentive ear to mask the grief of her lost dream, however she might have defined it. She loved him. She also knew he loved her, but he carried a heavier burden than their love could lift.

She feared that she would never see the passionate, beautiful son of de Catalan again. She suspected that she would later hear of a lost Templar falling to the King's soldiers, or drowning himself in unheralded despair.

Instead she heard another tale, one that made its rounds as fast as the missing ships of La Rochelle. It was the tale of a daring, wanted but unnamed sailor with a Templar crew that breached a southern port's defenses and tossed the King's soldiers overboard. That this mad captain, sword in hand, claimed the ship's helm, and proclaimed, "Until they release our brothers, and restore all that they have taken, we sail under the battle flag of the Knights Templar!"

His crew cheered, and hoisted up a black flag with a white skull and crossbones, what history now calls the Jolly Roger, or more commonly, the pirate flag.

In an infirmary, Pope Clement attended the former Inquisitor Robert, twitching on a bed. Destroyed.

Chancellor Nogaret paced in the outer room until Clement joined him, "You have your blessing, Chancellor. Prepare your ships."

Nogaret shook his head, "Your Holiness, I believe this is largely in your power to fix."

On the 6th of May in the Year of Our Lord 1312, another bull broached the lips of the town criers everywhere: "By papal decree: all former Templars must turn selves in to the church, for questioning and absolution. If they do not do so after one year, they are excommunicated. After another year, they are guilty of heresy with no right of appeal."

Barring heaven would draw the fugitives back to the king's control, so the Chancellor thought. Reports from England and Spain indicated that many lost Templars had already reclaimed their assurance by taking vows in other sacred orders, such as the Knights of the Hospital of Saint John.

But through France, the louder rumor spread of the black flagged vessel burning the sails of imperial ships, whose chests of treasure became a pirates' plunder and whose crews were set adrift to tell the tales, and report the losses.

King Philip sent his spies, and word returned of buried chests and reckless deeds on many a shore, from Gibraltar to Acre, from Genoa to Tunis, though none reported any from the seaport in Aragon, where old Simeon returned home after a long and uneventful day, until he was roped into the shadows.

"I know nothing!" Simeon squealed, "I am a peaceful man!"

Then he came face to face with Elias: "And we were bankers once. Come, we haven't much time before the next tide."

CHAPTER 27

In an upper room, the table sprawled with Simeon's books among Elias' maps, drawings, and his compass, all to serve the Baphomet ledger.

Simeon scratched his head as he ran his fingers over the strange text, "The first letters always indicate which cipher system to use. But these lines alternate: T, G, L, S... That's no pattern I know. I'm sorry."

Elias slouched, "But if you can't crack it..."

Outside, two crewmen stood guard. And from the darkness, a stone clapped stone, the crewmen looked, and an arrow struck one in the chest. Before he could fall, Noffo appeared behind the other, and silenced him with his dagger.

Noffo motioned into the darkness for his henchmen to replace the dead, while he crept in, and listened to the work from the upper room.

Past exhaustion, Elias absently stared at Baphomet on the ledger, and found Simeon doing the same. "You think we deserved this?"

Simeon snickered, and shifted in his seat.

"That is," Elias continued, "For all of our… What to call it now?... We were…" and his palms opened as if to say, "the hands of God in the world," but the words now seemed too much like a quaint memory, and foolish hubris, to say aloud. His eyes held on the ledger's impassable face of Baphomet, which still condemned his eternal soul.

Simeon let his thoughts settle: "I have many platitudes. But I have never been on a ship, or to the Holy Lands. I don't know. Some must have gone trying to serve God. Many used God to serve their greed. Not unlike your enemies. But judgment comes for us all, doesn't it? Maybe –"

"Baphomet is sitting on a round earth," Elias interrupted.

Simeon looked. The creature indeed stood on a round earth, and had multi-pointed stars on his forehead. Elias pulled out his compass and set it beside – his own star shaped compass was almost identical.

"He isn't the secret," Elias said, "He's the distraction." Elias cupped his hands over the star above Baphomet's head, "It's a wind-rose. Of course, those aren't cipher letters, they're compass points!"

Elias pointed to the first line of text: "Gerard said a sailor would understand! The first line 'T'... 'tramontana' – is Latin for North. That's the code! The ledger isn't a book; it's a map!"

Noffo's eyebrows raised as he sat, sword in his lap, and ate Simeon's dinner, while upstairs, Simeon brushed aside his other books and instruments and began plotting the compass initials in the ledger by Elias' instruction.

Elias pushed everything off the adjacent table and laid out his sailor's map.

"But where is the first point?" Simeon asked.

"Jerusalem. The center of any map."

Simeon examined the first line of text, and began his work. The rhythm of the cipher became clear and as Simeon unraveled the code, Elias plotted, drawing in longitudes and latitudes. He redrew certain points, plotting paths into the ocean, which made no sense. He shook his head, confused, but then continued marking.

By the turn of the next hour Elias had grown giddy, giggling to himself, urging Simeon on until he can't contain it. His hand pounded the table, "It can't be! It can't!"

"Read it yourself," Simeon said, looking up, "What are you so –?"

"Because it's not possible!"

Simeon stood and raised the lamp, and squinted down at Elias' lines that crossed the map of Europe and onto the table to the left, displaying an outline of Nova Scotia and parts of the Eastern seaboard. The New World.

"My God," Simeon muttered.

Elias beamed, "It's… as if the sun doesn't even rise or set."

Again he felt the tug of La Rochelle, the sea wind in his hair, and the taste of a land unspoiled. "I must prepare you for peace," the Grand Master said. Could it be that in such a world of miracles, God had devised yet another shore for their hearts, outside the clutch of kings and chancellors?

"No wonder they ran," Elias said, "Still, Molay should have said something."

Simeon sat back down, "I thought that was obvious. He sent you. He wanted you to know."

Elias nodded, "Corinne should see this. Both of you. You're both coming with me." But before Simeon could reply, Elias's face changed, "After I settle a certain debt in Paris."

"You wouldn't..." Simeon began, but Elias slowly reached over and took the lamp from Simon. Simeon turned.

Noffo stood by the stairs, with several rogues behind him.

Elias pulled the ledger shut on top of the map.

"After all this, would I make you go to Paris?" Noffo said, "Just hand over Baphomet."

Noffo waved Simeon away from the table with a flick of his sword, but Simeon shook his head in defiance, continuing to block the view.

"Whatever it is, it belongs to the king," Noffo continued, locking eyes with Elias.

Elias nodded... and smashed the lamp on the table.

The paperwork ignited in the oil bath. Noffo cried out and lunged, stabbing Simeon and plunging both their bodies toward the flame.

Elias flipped the table before Noffo reached it. Fire and burning paper scattered as Elias charged for the door.

He plunged down the stairs before the smoke consumed his breath. He wrestled against objects and opponents in the house, and finally crashed through a window into the near morning air.

And into the hands of rogues.

Elias fought, but they kicked out his feet and beat him down. And as Simeon's roof became a pyre, Noffo plunged through the front door, coughing smoke, angry, and empty-handed.

CHAPTER 28

At long last, the Bastille Prison opened its mighty gates for a handful of monks with cowls over their faces, escorting their prisoner on a wagon for interrogation:

Corinne.

The hearth crackled with glowing irons while Chancellor Nogaret stood by, fanning, and drinking himself into the mood.

Noffo sauntered in behind guards dragging Elias, his hands tied. They tossed a rope over a beam and hoisted his arms up.

"Come to confession, Templar." Nogaret said, setting the goblet down.

"Then you'll present me to the king?" Elias taunted, no doubt forced to listen to Noffo's ambitions all the way from Aragon, "How great is your reward, Noffo?"

Noffo struck Elias across the face.

The room waited as Elias lifted his head and addressed Nogaret: "If I tell..."

"You know I love your stories, captain," Nogaret teased.

"If I tell you, tonight," Elias said, "Tomorrow, you tell the King to restore the honor of the Templars... "

Nogaret looked around dramatically, "You mean me?"

"Repent before the Pope," Elias continued, "and release the Grand Master."

Nogaret savored the words, patting the leg stocks: "You. Really terrible at negotiation, but perhaps that comes with those vows. But you are stubborn. We'd hate to be the cause of any innocent person's suffering."

He opened the door and the monks dragged Corinne into the room. Elias called her name, but it wasn't until she saw Nogaret that she began to kick, bite, contort herself — anything to get away. Her arms slipped free but since she was barred from escape, she lunged at Nogaret, grappling his arm, and so upward, her nails barely missing his eyes.

The monks caught her up, and slammed her legs down in the stocks. She continued to struggle, still clinging to Nogaret's arm, until monks pried her arms away. She managed to snatch up the wine goblet from the table, but before she could wield or even spill it, the monks restrained her, holding it upright.

The moment was too delicious for the Chancellor. His eyes flitted back and forth from the sailor to the lover, until their eyes found each other.

Then Nogaret took the goblet from her hand as if she had served it, and drank: "Everything is made known in time. Laid bare to the truth."

He set the goblet aside and removed Corinne's shoes, almost seductively, exposing her tender feet. He made sure the tied former Templar could see him tickle her instep and make her squirm, "Laid bare. Even Molay must make a public confession to keep himself out of the king's dungeons. But what would you tell me, Elias de Catalan?"

Elias kept his gaze on Corinne, knowing that his secrets were at an end.

The nearest cowl covered monk grabbed a hot iron from the fire and showed it to Elias. Elias glanced down first, but then nodded to himself inwardly, and looked up into the man's face, and blinked with disbelief.

He turned back to Corinne. "Very well," Elias said, his courage rising, "Then for your crimes, I stand to defend the honor of my order. I challenge you to judicial combat."

The guards laughed. And after a beat, Nogaret joined in and said, "There are no Templars, excommunicate."

The monk kicked Noffo back, and pressed the hot iron into Elias' rope — searing through it.

The cowl slipped back revealing Hugh. The other Templars brandished steel from their monk's garb and drove back the prison guards.

One tossed a Templar sword to Elias, who turned on the Chancellor: "Let God decide."

Elias bounded over the table as Nogaret turned and ducked through the open door.

Corinne called out, "No, Elias! Wait!"

But Elias went hunting, chasing Nogaret through chamber after chamber. In each, the clamor rose and more guards awoke. The Templars and Corinne were soon in full retreat, battling soldiers behind them and in front.

Hugh thundered through the corridors after Elias, losing his way along one turn, and switching back. He turned a corner too quickly, and ran into Noffo's sword. Noffo leaned in but Hugh was stronger, and extracting the blade while backing him up.

Other Templars rushed in, driving Noffo back with flashes of their swords while Hugh retreated, painfully, and bloody.

Nogaret burst into the night air, with slow, labored breathing toward the Bastille gate. He spit curses for guards to stop the Templar pirate rogue who stole the king's money, but before him stood only a stunned valet.

Nogaret's breath came short. He coughed hard, and still pushed onward. The valet reached for him but Nogaret's legs buckled, stumbling. He spit up a dark liquid that did not taste of his own blood, but of the wine. And something else.

Nogaret struggled to focus on the Bastille gate, and fell at his valet's feet.

The lad fled as Elias charged up and stood over Nogaret in horror as his foe's tongue lapped for air like a dying animal: "No! Get up! Don't you cheat me!"

Elias' mind raced back to moments before, to Corinne's contortions in the stocks, snatching the goblet, and holding it upright as Templars disguised as monks held it upright so it would not spill. How calm then did Corinne's face seem as Nogaret snatched the goblet back, and how satisfied when he drank. Then Elias remembered her words from the voyage, "I could get close enough, like this. Close enough to poison him..."

Nogaret's tongue curled, and dangled like a lifeless dog, as all the rest of his functions ceased.

A moment later, Corinne was at Elias' arm as Templars dragged Hugh out and onto a wagon: "Get in!"

Elias pulled away, "You cheated us!"

"I did it for you!" Her mind also raced back to the voyage: "You're not meant for –"

Elias snatched up Corinne and hurled her onto the wagon. The Templars paused, expecting him to climb on as well but as the whip drove the horse forward, Elias shewed them away.

Corinne held onto Hugh with one hand and beckoned Elias with the other.

Elias waved back with his sword, "I won't live condemned! The king is also a knight!"

And with that, he ran off into the darkness.

CHAPTER 29

On the 18th day of March in the Year of Our Lord, 1314, Parisians jostled for a spot in the public square to hear one final confession.

Nogaret had told the truth. The disgraced Jacque de Molay, along with Geoffroi de Charnay, former Preceptor of Normandy, the final leaders of the Poor Knights of the Temple of Solomon, were buying back their souls.

No one knew that Pope had resolved to commute their life sentences, perhaps within a few months, so that they might live out their days in an obscure monastery.

The men sat silently beside the row of sour-faced cardinals on the podium, while at the Parliament office across the public square, King Philip watched like a Roman emperor, surrounded by attendants. On other balconies through the building, various officials and clerics gathered, and with them, a well-dressed Florian, forever ingratiating himself.

Archbishop Sens addressed the crowd for nearly half an hour, expounding on the abuses that the late Chancellor had levied against the order seven years ago, along with the account of the order's just punishment: "... to which you are all witnesses."

In the crowd, Corinne searched, her shawl pressed against her face to hide her features. She glanced away from the French guards to avoid detection, and came within a few yards of Noffo, also searching. She shrank behind others and skulked away, moving closer to the scaffold, where the Archbishop continued:

"The Grand Master and Preceptor of Normandy will confess the extent of their infamy, absolving themselves, and so receive the due mercy of the church."

But before Molay stood, the Archbishop picked up the cruel chorus once again: "Others continue to defy God, and their condemnation is pronounced. Harbor none of them. Offer no sanctuary. No absolution. No mercy."

Molay winced at each phrase, and then with Charnay's help, stood, and took a step toward the crowd. He glanced toward the King on his perch far across the square, and then upward.

Then his jaw went slack...

Upon the roof, his wayward charge, the infamous Elias de Catalan tied off a rope and glared down upon the French crown. If the once great Grand Master intended to condemn them one last time, and in public, Elias would answer, to avenge his order and his soul.

Corinne noticed Molay's expression and turned to look.

In looking, Noffo spotted her in the crowd and reflexively turned, also spying the "Little Assassin!"

He raced through the sea of humanity toward the offices while on the scaffold, the Archbishop prodded Molay to speak.

Molay shuffled to his mark, still distracted. The wind blew, pressing his tunic against his bones, and the Parisians gasped in one accord. Was this the man whose knights paraded and riddles rapt their children's delight before that fateful Friday the thirteenth?

"Before heaven and earth," Molay began, testing his quivering voice against the murmuring crowd, "And with all of you here as my witnesses, I confess... I am indeed guilty… Of the greatest infamy."

He barely managed to spit forth the words, though he had rehearsed them past all revulsion. But above the waiting, ignorant crowd and the deceiving crown, Elias donned his Templar vestment, the red cross upon a field of white.

Molay watched as Elias checked his rope, weighed his sword in hand, and readied himself to descend. Then with one last pause, Elias glanced toward his Grand Master, perhaps for spite, or else for permission.

On the scaffold, Molay's eyes widened as his voice rose, "But the infamy is...that I have lied."

The cardinals nodded, approving, assuming he meant his denied confession.

"I have lied by admitting these disgusting charges," Molay clarified, "I declare, I must declare, that the order is innocent! Its purity and saintliness is beyond question!"

The Cardinals stumbled, starting to rise, while the clerics on the balconies hissed and the King flared his nostrils.

And Elias halted.

"I indeed confessed to what my enemies wanted," Molay went on, "To save myself from their terrible tortures..."

The Archbishop directed his guards but they were too far from the Grand Master, rising to his full breath: "Other knights who retracted their confessions have been burned at the stake! Yet I shall not confess to foul crimes which have never been committed..."

Elias' breath came short, the words piercing:

"Life is offered to me but at the price of infamy. At such a price, life is not worth having. Do not grieve my death if life can be bought only by piling one lie upon another."

The crowd jeered loudly – some at Molay – though many at the King!

Corinne teared up, looked toward the roof, praying, willing the words to rest in Elias' ear as former hymns had steadied him. The great lie had been broken.

Geofrroi de Charnay stepped forward, his hand on his old friend's shoulder and there he spoke with similar defiance, though his words were not recorded. Perhaps no one heard them in all the commotion.

Nor did Elias know yet what this new confession meant, but he let go of his rope.

And as he turned, a blade flashed, cutting Elias' shoulder — Noffo on the attack!

Elias toppled, grasping the rope again as he slid from the roof.

Below him, King Philip the Fair rose, uttering no more than this to his attendants: "Burn them."

His attendants rushed off, as he shook his head in disgust, while just above, Elias swung awkwardly, and after a bounce against the frame, crashed through the window into Nogaret's old office.

It seemed he barely had a moment to brush away the splintered glass before Noffo kicked open the side door, his blade flashing in the poor light.

Elias first flung the curtains, then the nearest books toward his attacker, evading blows as he fought to reach the main door.

"I've earned Baphomet, you heretic!" Noffo thundered, "You're going to the king with me!"

"The king doesn't even know you!" Elias spat back.

And so the Templar and the pirate clashed, tearing through the room. They slipped on the littered papers, crossed swords and clenched at the door, their blades carving a scrawl into the wood.

Elias kicked Noffo back, flung open the door and dove, barely evading Noffo's slashing. Then in the hall, Elias rolled to the railing, his sword protecting against Noffo's lunge, then he grappling him, and pulled him down.

The pirate elbowed Elias with his free hand, but as he pulled his sword hand loose, Elias rose up and yanked hard on the rope beside the hall window, crashing the thick curtain down over Noffo.

He quickly looped the rope around Noffo's shoulders, and leapt off the railing, swinging down toward the next landing.

Noffo's blade pulled free from the curtain and chopped the rope against the rail.

Elias thudded onto the floor below, expunging all his breath. His head rang, disrupting his senses, and blood ran from his nose. He blinked, gasping, and stretched out his aching arm toward his sword, which had bounced well out of reach.

Noffo bounded down the stairs to the landing while nearby footsteps grew louder in his ears. Noffo knew the king would enter the hall at any of his next successive breaths and he would be ready to present him with such an appropriate gift.

He dragged Elias up, pressing his sword to Elias' neck, "You're only hope of heaven is to give the King everything! You Templars are over!"

But as the king's attendants opened the chamber door, Elias feigned his throat into Noffo's blade, and whispered "Our hope is in God."

Noffo instinctively loosened, not wanting to present his king a corpse, and Elias dropped, tucking his chin and shoving Noffo forward.

Thus, plunging through the frail attendants Noffo stumbled into the king's presence alone, sword in hand. The King's attendants dove on Noffo, heedless of Elias escape toward the nearest staircase.

"Is there no end to this villainy?" The king sang, "Hang him, within the hour!"

Noffo began, "Your majesty – your majesty!" That was as far as his protest went before guards hammered him into silence.

Elias flung his vestment behind him, abandoned his sword, and as he reached the stairs came face to face with Florian. The cleric, now in comfortable possession of land south of Paris, clutched his finery, as if to beg, "Don't kill me!"

Elias shoved past him without a thought, down and into the street, and collapsed into Corinne's arms.

"Molay!" He huffed, struggling to right his quivering frame.

Corinne threw her shawl over him and helped him through the crowd.

Though he wanted to outrun the king's command, to rescue and abscond with his former master, his flesh delayed him, and ultimately, it refused to obey.

As the sun set on the riverside, Elias and Corinne sat on the stones along with hundreds of the curious as soldiers wrestled Molay and Charnay into a boat. They cast off the lines that moored them, and rowed across the Seine to a small island in the shadow of Notre Dame.

They dragged the last two Templars to a single pile of wood that surrounded a single stake, as Molay kicked and cursed: "They've destroyed thousands, waged wars for their own profit and pride! Heaping evil on evil!"

A torch set off the kindling. The flames burned quickly, lapping up the wood and searing the rope and vestments and the men.

By Notre Dame, many turned their heads in shame, but a young priest continued to stare and took tentative steps toward the Seine as Molay pulled one hand free and shook it back at Paris: "I call the King and Pope to meet me before the throne of God! Before the year's end!"

The flames lashed their face, unbearable. Charnay's final words rang, "Spes mea in Deo est!" The greatest Templar motto: My hope is in God.

Then as the flames overcame the Grand Master, his words were: "Vekam, Adonai!" Hebrew for "Revenge, O Lord!" and he fainted.

And by the shore, Elias' eyes burned with tears as Corinne held him.

"What now, love?" She said.

Elias shook his head, and in that motion saw the young priest watching, also with tearful eyes that glinted from the distant fire.

Elias motioned with his chin, and Corinne helped Elias to his feet, and he began to speak...

By the morn, in a small chapel, the penitent Elias knelt before the altar and received communion from the young priest – both men still in tears. "The blood of Christ has absolved you of all sin," the priest delivered, "That in the last day you might stand before him blameless and with exceeding joy. Go in peace, brother."

Corinne helped Elias up: "So are you free now?"

Elias shook his head, a smile spreading, "I have a whole new world to show you."

So at long last, Elias de Catalan took his lady to sea. Upon a Carrack, warm from Tunis, and stocked with provisions, Elias captained a crew as loyal and as pious as the warrior monks they once were. They bowed with souls unburdened as the ship's priest blessed their vessel, their voyage, and the sacred union of Elias and Corinne, as they sailed into the West.

CONCLUSION

On the night of March 18, 1314, several Paris priests swam across the river and took away the bones Jacque de Molay and Geoffroi de Charnay as holy relics.

A month later, on April 20, Pope Clement died in his bed of stomach cancer.

Then on November 29, in that same year, King Philip IV also died, after a hunting accident.

Of Hugh Von Grumbach and the other Templars that vanished in the forests of Vienne, most were never seen again. Those who confessed lived out their lives in church sanctuary. Others disappeared into other religious orders, or fought for their cause of justice on land and on the high seas. As we know, their battle flag of the skull and crossbones became a different symbol in the coming age.

However, some historians speculate that the Templars did indeed prevail in recovering their wealth and founding a country of their own. Decipher if you will: lay a finger down on any map and follow the lines south of Vienne. Or consider what reputation a nation might earn whose founders were known for secrecy and banking. Or simply invert the Templar vestment from a red cross on a white field to one with of a white cross on a red field, to reveal the flag of Switzerland.

The End

ABOUT THE AUTHOR

Bren is a screenwriter and story analyst who has written scripts in various genres, provided coverage for production companies, provided script analysis for nearly 100 screenwriters from around the world, and mentored several towards the completion of their stories.

His website, www.bren.us, provides insights into screenwriting, movies and culture.

OTHER WORKS BY BRENNAN SMITH

WITTENBERG

As Denmark declares another military victory over Sweden, in quiet Wittenberg, Germany, a scarred Swedish soldier, Galen, dares to win his

Princess Margaret's love by conspiring to kidnap Prince Hamlet. But what they don't know is that Hamlet's brother Valdemar has come in secret to woo and marry Margaret to ratify the peace!

Plots converge to murder and bloody indulgence on the streets as Martin Luther prepares for Lent, 1517.

For those with a passion for Shakespeare comes a prequel to Shakespeare's Hamlet. Yes, this is full 5-Act play in iamic pentameter, complete with sword fights, monologues, and many twists. Also known as Bren's "Hamlet meets Martin Luther" story, Wittenberg was performed in New York City in 2004 to the wonder of audiences who loved its mix of Shakespearean romance, comedy and history.

EXTRAS

This Kindle ebook also contains chapters on:

- "The Tale of Two Wittenbergs" - the author's journey to develop the story through his research in Wittenberg, Germany, and Stratford-on-Avon and London, UK
- How to write like Shakespeare
- Considerations for staging Wittenberg, including casting and technical requirements
- A Wittenberg plot summary
- Other fragments of the author's poetry practice

54017489R00095

Made in the USA
San Bernardino, CA
05 October 2017